THE SPIRIT

FOR JOHN

The Spirit Of Ganesh

SLUM KIDS OF CALCUTTA

Maureen Roberts

YOUCAXTON PUBLICATIONS
OXFORD & SHREWSBURY

ISBN 978-1-911175-57-5
Printed and bound in Great Britain.
Published by YouCaxton Publications 2017

YouCaxton Publications
enquiries@youcaxton.co.uk

Contents

1

Rupa Learns to Rat-Catch

The dim light of a street lamp shines down a narrow alleyway, faintly revealing a shifting movement amongst the dumped rubbish. A twitching nose pokes from a crevice in the crumbling brick wall. A long thin tail vanishes down a hole. Black furry bodies furtively scurry about. Here live the rats. This is their world. In holes, in pipes and in the walls of the alleyway, they hide themselves away during daytime and slyly emerge, only when the darkness falls.

Their home is this alleyway, in this city, in this vast country of India. A country which is home to millions of rats... and millions of people.

The heavy rain had ceased and the stench of rotting food wafted hot and steamy, into the quivering nostrils of the hungry rats. Invigorated by the evening's heat and humidity and their need for food, the rats emerge. With muffled squealing's and squeaking's, they scurry up and down the alleyway, gorging on food scraps, thrown over the wall from a nearby café. Soon the filthy floor is covered in a heaving mass of hairy bodies.

A broken barrier straddled the end of the alleyway that opened onto a busy street. A boney cow wandering along tried to get in. It butted its head against the barrier which tilted and almost fell flat. The cow made a half-hearted attempt to jump over, but gave up. Munching on a mouldy cabbage stalk, it slowly sauntered off.

A few minutes went by, then another shadowy movement faintly flickered on the wall at the street end of the alley. Peeping round the corner and squinting down the dark passage appeared a skinny little girl. She stared fixedly at the ground, gave a small gasp of surprise and ducked back behind the wall. The rats took no notice; they were too busy in their frenzy of feeding.

Rupa is eight. Her long black hair is scraped back into a tight pigtail and secured with an elastic band. Her sharp little face frowns in concentration as she clutches a plastic sack with one hand and holds a wooden stick tightly in the other. Cautiously, she leans forward and peers once again down the alley.

"Ugh!! There are hundreds," she whispers fearfully to her friend Samira, "I'm not sure I can do this job!"

Samira furiously whispers back, "You're a rat – catcher's deputy Rupa and you agreed. I showed you what to do, now let's get going!" She gives her a hard push.

Rupa pulls a face and leaps over the barrier. Her bare feet are sucked into the black filth. Frantically whacking and jabbing at the black hairy bodies, she attempts to knock them senseless. The rats squeal loudly and scatter. In a second the alleyway is deserted.

"Not like that," hissed Samira, "That was a stupid thing to do Rupa. We'll never catch any if you go at it like that."

Samira shook her head crossly and scowled. She was a big girl of about eleven, with a chubby round face and a surprisingly little pointy nose. Her hair was cut short in uneven hanks and in some places stuck up in black tufts. Like Rupa, she was wearing an ill-fitting, dirty dress and like Rupa she was barefoot.

"Now listen to me Rupa and remember this time," she grumbled impatiently. Rupa avoided looking at her.

"I've got to shine this torch into their eye first. Rupa are you listening?" she repeated, pinching Rupa's arm spitefully. Rupa shrank away from her.

"When they are staring at the light, you bash them with the stick. Now do it properly." To emphasise the point she pinched poor Rupa once again.

Rupa looked fearfully at Samira and rubbed at her painful arm. She needed this job, so she had to do it right.

Samira crept down the passage, her eyes peering at the filthy ground. Rupa followed, keeping close to Samira. Samira spotted a gap between the bricks of the end wall. She flicked on the torch. Rupa stared and held her breath. They waited.

Out from the space between the bricks poked a curious furry face. Its whiskers trembled. It was staring at the torchlight.

"Now Rupa! Now!"

Rupa raised her stick and brought it down, with as much power as she could; crack on the rat's head. The rat fell off the wall onto the ground and staggered up onto its wobbly legs.

"Again!" screamed Samira, "Bash it again!"

Rupa made frantic stabs at the rat and then holding the stick with both hands, dealt it a blow which lifted it off the ground and sailed it through the air. It fell onto a heap of discarded plastic, gave a shudder and lay still.

Rupa put her hands on the wall and was sick all down it.

"You did well," laughed Samira staring at her. She shrugged her shoulders. "Everyone feels sick the first time. You'll soon get used to it."

She picked the battered rat up by its tail and dumped it into the sack.

"That's one. We have to catch twenty nine more; else the rat-catcher will give the job to somebody else."

They stood still once again. This time their keen ears detected movement under some wet newspapers. Samira snatched the wooden stick off Rupa and ran at the newspaper.

Whack! Whack! Whack!!

She thumped the paper with all her strength, lifting the stick high over her head and belting the paper. Whack! Whack! Again and again the stick hit the paper. Samira, out of breath, stood panting and staring at the sodden newspaper. It slowly turned a ghastly colour of red. Bending down she lifted up a corner of the paper. In a mangled mass lay four dead rats.

Rupa, once more, leaned against the wall and threw up.

"You're going to be no good if you keep being sick," said Samira angrily as she picked up each rat and dropped it in the sack.

"I'll be alright in a minute" faltered Rupa suppressing another nauseous wave, "It's just that they look so horrible. "

"Don't look then, "retorted Samira. "Come on, this time you shine the torch and I'll whack them."

She gave the torch to Rupa. Rupa switched it on and pointed the beam at a broken drainpipe. Up, from a hole in the middle, appeared a large black rat. It gazed unblinkingly into the torch light. Rupa's hand shook as she stared at its bright red eyes. Then she shut her eyes tightly, as the stick came down and bashed the rat back into the pipe. Samira gave a shout of triumph and shook the pipe. A huge dead rat fell out of one end, followed by a heap of hairless wriggling babies.

Rupa thought she was going to faint. She leaned on the wall, as Samira flung the dead rat into the sack. Samira then bent down and shovelled all the babies onto a piece of cardboard. Grinning at Rupa, she walked to a deep puddle by the barrier at the end of the alleyway and dropped them in. They paddled around piteously in a blind panic, as a horrified Rupa watched.

"They don't count," said Samira bossily. "We don't get paid for babies. They'll drown soon and be out of their misery. Now how many have we got?"

Ten rats later Samira decided they had caught enough for one night.

"We'll carry on tomorrow," she said, "and take them to the rat-catcher. Oh look Rupa! Those baby rats are still swimming around."

Rupa felt like weeping as she avoided looking at the struggling rat babies.

They walked slowly towards their homes, Samira slinging the heavy sack over her shoulder and Rupa carrying the torch and stick.

At the end of the row of shops and cafes was the main highway into the centre of the huge city.

In spite of their burdens, the two girls ran expertly across the busy road, dodging the lorries, buses and cars.

Across the road was the slum area where both girls lived. Thousands of homemade shacks piled up against each other. Remove but one and it seemed as if they would all topple down.

Planks of wood and corrugated iron were jig-sawed together to make walls. Some shacks had tiles on the roof but most were made from layers of plastic weighted down by bricks or old car tyres. Floors were of flattened earth and most shacks contained only sleeping mats and a few cooking utensils. There was no electricity or water in these poor hovels. Paraffin lamps provided some light and buckets were used to fetch water from a stand pipe. A row of smelly, fly infested toilets were used by hundreds of people. Many just squatted down over the open drains that ran down the middle of the narrow lanes.

Even at this late hour, the place was a hive of activity. The noise of people busy in tiny workshops, banging, sawing, hammering and sewing intermingled with voices laughing, talking, singing and shouting. Radios were turned on at full blast. Smells of cooking, incense, heating oil and other not very pleasant odours floated along the tiny passages. Disregard the muted cries, the coughing and the muffled angry voice and this place appeared like a friendly haven, safe from the frightening, bigger world of the city.

Samira lived a few shacks away from Rupa. At one side of Rupa's home was a small gap where Rupa's Dad used to store his re-cycling finds. Two worn tyres and some pieces of rusty car engine were barely visible.

"Can we hide the rats up here Rupa? We'll collect them tomorrow when we've caught the others."

"Won't they get pongy? We might poison everyone."

"Don't be stupid Rupa. We're only leaving them for one night. They won't start a plague."

Samira shoved the sack into the gap.

"Is your Mother back yet?"

Rupa shook her head, "I don't think so. She catches a late bus back from the city"

"Well let's go and see if Mr Chopra will give us some chai. I'm so thirsty."

"OK, but let me just wash myself Samira, I feel filthy."

Outside Rupa's shack was a plastic bucket filled with water. Rupa scooped up the water in a small jug and poured it over her hands. She splashed it onto her face and tipped the remains over her feet. Wiping her face vigorously with the edge of her skirt, she rushed to catch up with Samira.

2

Samira Takes on the 'Big Boys'

Samira was hurrying up the lane towards a shack with an open front and bamboo mats on the floor.

Mr Chopra was a fat, little man with strands of orange, henna – dyed hair plastered over his round scalp. Rupa had often wondered how his strands stayed flat on his bare head. She came to the conclusion, that he must use special glue to keep them in place. The tea shop was part of Mr Chopra's house, which consisted of the open – fronted shop and an upper floor where he, his wife and three children lived. Mr Chopra was considered a fortunate man; he had a two roomed house which was taller than all the others in the row. Mr Chopra didn't consider himself fortunate. He had a thin, disgruntled wife, two daughters aged twelve and thirteen and a son aged seven. The son went to a school under the railway arches. His Father was very proud of him. The girls stayed at home, gazing enviously at the Bollywood stars on their battered television set.

There was much wailing and shouting coming from the shop as Rupa and Samira arrived. Mr Chopra was yelling at his daughters and the unhappy girls were sobbing and attempting to hide behind their Mother.

"It's a great opportunity, the money is good, you will be working in a big house and the man said you can come back to visit us."

The girls moaned and clung closer to their Mother.

Mr Chopra continued shouting, "You are big girls now, you can work. There is nothing for you here. How can one tea shop support five people? Besides I've agreed and the man has given me the money to clinch the deal."

Mr Chopra shrugged his shoulders in exasperation, then turned away as if to say these were his final words on the matter,

Rupa and Samira stared at the wailing girls. Rupa thought they were lucky to be getting jobs and she whispered to Samira,

"At least it won't be rat catching."

"Could be much worse," muttered Samira, as they watched the wretched girls scuttle upstairs with their Mother.

"What do you two want?" Mr Chopra turned from frowning at his daughters and instead frowned at Rupa and Samira.

"And what have you two been up to? Look at your filthy frocks. You are both a disgrace."

"We've been working Mr Chopra," retorted Samira, tossing her head and pursing her lips. "We're not idle and lazy."

"You've been working for that rat-catcher again?"

"So!?" Samira lifter her eyebrows and put her hand on her hip.

"Everybody knows he's a drunkard. He'll be sacked from his job one of these days." Mr Chopra suddenly laughed, "You could take over."

"I'm not going to be a rat – catcher," blurted out Rupa, "It's a horrible job."

"Too right my dear," agreed Mr Chopra. "It's a nasty occupation and not for young girls." He paused, wiped his hands on his shirt then continued; "Now my girls have got good jobs working for rich families."

He paused again and seemed lost in worried thoughts. He put his hand to his head and closed his eyes.

Samira gave a loud cough. Mr Chopra opened his eyes quickly saying impatiently,

"What do you two want?" without waiting for an answer he continued, "I suppose you want some tea?"

"Yes please, Mr Chopra," wheedled Samira in a false sweet voice, "but can we pay you tomorrow?"

"Can you pay tomorrow?" Mr Chopra wearily repeated. "That's what they all say." He seemed momentarily distracted again, but pulling himself upright said, "OK! Don't forget!"

He went to the back of the shack, lifted a kettle off a small kerosene stove and poured out two glasses of milky tea. He set them down on a low table and Rupa and Samira sat cross-legged on the mat beside it. They sipped the tea slowly, distracted by the sounds of muted whimpers and moaning's coming from above.

"I can't stand this!" burst out Mr Chopra suddenly. He stomped angrily upstairs and the cries ceased.

"Samira! Samira!"

An urgent whisper interrupted the girls. A plump, nearly naked little boy of about four with a very snotty nose and three equally snotty little friends appeared at the front of the shop. They all stood with their fingers in their mouths, squirming about and staring at Samira and Rupa.

"Samira, Samira."

Impatiently, Samira pulled a face at the fattest one. Baljit was the youngest of her three brothers. He had a very round belly and was wearing shorts several sizes too big. Samira heaved a sigh.

"What do you want Baljit? You should be at home asleep."

Baljit ignored this and started to whine pathetically,

"Samira." His big eyes filled with tears as he blurted out, "The big boys took my marbles."

His little friends shuffled their bare feet and grizzled in sympathy, squinting up cunningly at the exasperated Samira. Samira stared at them. Raising her eyes upwards she asked curiously,

"Your marbles?"

The quartet nodded, tears and snot intermingled.

"Well you shouldn't play with the big boys," she scolded, "You are too little."

She turned to Rupa and muttered, "I'm never free of them. Always wanting something."

But then she repented and turned back to them. Baljit stood waiting patiently his big brown eyes fixed expectantly on his big sister.

"Oh all right," she pulled a cross face. "Where are they?"

"Down there Samira, near our place," Baljit's tears miraculously stopped.

"OK. I'm coming"

Samira heaved herself reluctantly up from the mat, slurped the dregs of her tea, waved to Mr Chopra, who had appeared from upstairs and set off, at a purposeful trot, down the lane. Rupa and the little boys ran to keep up with her.

Dodging the dogs, hens, rubbish and people, Samira spotted and made for a group of teenagers playing marbles. Before they could stop her she stormed over to a hole in the ground and scooped up all the marbles lying there. She also picked up several from the ground.

"Hey! What are you doing?"

A big, scrawny lad grabbed Samira's arm. Samira rounded on him and shook him off.

"Don't you ever pinch little kids' marbles again," she yelled in his face.

He backed away, "We won them. They wanted to play."

"Don't give me that! Look how little they are. They don't know how to play."

The four little kids pressed up to her, staring at the big boys with frowny faces and lips pushed out.

Samira looked down at them angrily, "And don't you

four go playing with anymore big kids. Stick with little ones. Now take them and go home."

The four snatched the marbles out of her open hands and scarpered off grinning at each other.

"Remember!" she scowled at the big lads, "You take advantage of them again and I'll have you."

They all looked at the ground and shuffled away mumbling and throwing her angry looks.

Rupa gazed admiringly at Samira

"That was great Samira. You're not afraid of anyone."

"I am though Rupa," said Samira suddenly serious. "That man who gave Mr Chopra some money for his daughters doesn't sound right. Supposing he comes for me?"

"He won't Samira. You've got a job with the rat – catcher and you give the money to your Dad."

"Yes! But supposing the rat-catcher loses his job? What then?"

But Samira had reached her shack and before Rupa could think of a reply she said,

"Taraah Rupa. See you tomorrow, same place," and she slipped inside.

3

The Fortune Teller

R upa's shack was empty. A long time ago, Rupa's Father had gone away to work at the big ship yard. Memories of being lifted high in the air and hugged by strong arms were all Rupa had left of him. The money, he occasionally managed to send, soon stopped and he never came back home. Rupa's Mother took to sitting in a corner of the shack and crying. Then one day she went out early, found a job in the city and never spoke of him again.

Although it was now very late her Mother had not yet returned. Rupa felt hungry. There was no food in the food box, so she curled up on her sleeping mat to wait. She was woken from a doze by a small thin woman shaking her shoulder.

"Rupa, wake up! You've not had your supper and I've brought you some food."

Rupa sleepily roused herself.

"Mum, you are so late and I'm starving," she yawned.

"I'm sorry 'm late lovey. Mr and Mrs Rai had a dinner party this evening and look, I've brought us some leftovers."

She opened a carrier bag and lifted out several plastic containers. Wonderful aromatic curry smells floated towards Rupa.

"Now can you run along to the chapatti maker and buy four chapattis?"

She gave Rupa a few coins and Rupa dashed off.

It took no time at all to eat all the delicious food. Rupa mopped up the juices with pieces of hot chapatti. She nibbled on chicken, fish pieces and vegetables. All the containers were scraped clean. Everything was eaten and the containers washed in the water bucket outside.

Rupa felt so full, she flopped back on her mat and looked at her Mother curiously.

"What do you do at Mrs Rai's house Mum?"

Rupa's Mum smiled tiredly and pushed back her straggly, greying hair.

"Well let's see. I scrub floors, sweep the paths, peel the vegetables, scour the pans, wash up, run errands and do whatever I am told to do."

"Mr Chopra's daughters are going away to work at a big house."

Rupa's Mum looked at her sharply, "How do you know that?"

"They were crying and Mr Chopra told us. He said a man had given him some money. Samira is scared that she might have to go too. I won't have to go will I Mum?"

Her Mum leaned over and held her tightly,

"Never! Never! Nobody will take you away from me. Now tuck yourself down and sleep. I've left a chapatti in the box for your breakfast."

When Rupa woke next morning her Mother had already left for work.

Later, after she had eaten, Rupa went out into the lane. It was already filled with busy people trying to earn some money. Tiny stalls were selling flowers, food and trinkets of all kinds. Who would buy this stuff Rupa wondered. Children were racing down the alleys chasing various animals. Ducks, chickens and pigs all scattered to safety on roofs, under ledges or launched themselves clumsily to the skies. Was that Baljit and his little gang? Some kids were squatting in the gutter, playing their own secret games involving stones, pieces of string or bits of sticks. Rupa banged on the door of the shack next to hers. An elderly woman carrying a bucket opened the door and handed the bucket to Rupa. Rupa banged on the door of the next shack. Again the door was opened and a bucket thrust at her. Rupa then trotted down the lane to a standpipe which supplied water for hundreds of households. There was a long queue of people waiting patiently with their buckets. It seemed like hours to Rupa, before her turn came. She carefully brimmed her buckets with the precious water and staggered back.

She repeated this three times for different households and each time received a few coins. The fourth time, as she was staggering back up the lane, she noticed Samira in front of her. Samira was also carrying two buckets filled with water. Rupa was just about to shout to her when a gang of boys charged down the lane. They all deliberately barged into Samira and knocked her flying. Water cascaded everywhere. The boys hooted with laughter.

"Serve you right for stealing from us," they shrieked in her face and ran off.

Samira was sitting in the middle of the street, with a dazed look and a sopping wet dress when Rupa reached her.

"I'm so fed up with this," muttered Samira, her fists clenched, "I'm fed up with waiting for water, catching filthy rats and living in this place." Her face looked strained and grim.

"Take my buckets Samira," said Rupa gently. "I've already seen to everyone, these were for Mum and me. I'll fill them again later."

Samira wearily stood up, the skirt of her dress plastered in dirt.

"Thanks Rupa. I will take them and I'll meet you outside your house in a minute."

Rupa looked worriedly at her and picked up the emptied buckets.

The girls spent the afternoon hanging round various little workshops. They delivered tea, swept floors, picked up scrap and materials, ran errands for various people and pushed a cart, laden with bits of wood from the woodyard, down to the carpenters shack.

Then each happily jingling a pocket full of coins, they set off home to continue their rat catching.

On the way back Rupa spotted a fortune teller. She was sitting on a small veranda, surrounded by excited people. What an exotic old woman! Her head was covered by a richly embroidered purple shawl and she was tiny, not much bigger than Rupa. Silver earrings and silver nose rings adorned her dark, wrinkled, ancient face. Her beady little eyes were heavily outlined in thick black kohl.

Rupa nudged Samira, "Look!"

The fortune teller was peering at a set of cards and by her side was a wire cage with a parrot in it.

"Let's watch her," whispered Samira. "I'd love to have my fortune told Rupa."

They wriggled through the crowd to the front. A worried looking woman was about to have her fate revealed. The fortune teller held up some cards with one claw-like hand and undid the cage door with the other. The parrot busily hopped out and pecked at a card which the fortune teller then read. The worried woman's face relaxed and looked pleased. The parrot was shoved back into its cage.

A man pushed forward and handed over a few coins. The cage was again opened. The parrot emerged, hesitated, then with a clumsy flapping of short, clipped wings made a frantic dash for freedom. It ran round and round the outside of its cage, then hopped on top of it. Scrabbling its way up the side of an adjacent shack it got onto the roof. There it perched, bright green and looking very pleased with itself. It cocked its head on one side and peered curiously down at the upturned astonished faces.

The fortune teller leapt to her little feet, shouting and waving the cage frantically at the bird. It took no notice. Someone in the crowd started to laugh. Soon all the crowd was laughing. The parrot strutted up and down, cawing loudly in a 'show off' manner. Then it stopped to preen its feathers and scratch its beak. The noise of laughter caught its attention. It leaned down from the roof, opened its beak wide and cackled loud and long. The crowd were in hysterics.

"I'll try to catch it for you", volunteered Rupa, on seeing the fortune teller's distraught face. She nimbly hoisted herself up the wooden wall of the shack and peeped over the roof. The parrot was hopping gleefully up and down and merrily squawking at the crowd. The excited crowd was very merrily squawking back.

It seemed a shame to stop the fun. Rupa turned and grinned down at Samira who pulled a scary face back at her. She turned slowly and fixed her eyes on the merry parrot. The parrot had its back to her. Slowly, slowly she inched forward holding her breath. Then with a huge lunge she stretched full out and caught the parrot's leg. Surprised, it turned round, gave a shriek and pecked her hand hard. Rupa held on grimly as the parrot made repeated stabs at her. She edged backward and clambered down the wall, holding fast to the frenzied bundle of feathers and its scrawny, scaly leg. Its furious owner reached out and yanking it by the neck stuffed it feet first, squawking and flapping back into its cage. Mournfully it looked out at Rupa, its big yellow eyes staring accusingly at her.

The fortune teller was delighted, "I'll tell your fortune for free dearie," she beamed, showing long brown stained teeth.

"No not me!" Rupa was a bit frightened of her and shy at all the attention she was getting.

"Tell my friend's fortune, she'd like that."

"Where's your friend then?"

Samira pushed herself forward and sat in front of the fortune teller.

"I'm not risking using my parrot dearie. Give me your hands and I'll read your palm."

Samira held out both hands. The fortune teller leaned forward and grasped them. She stoked Samira's hands bent back her thumbs and fingers and scrutinised Samira's palms.

"Hard worked hands," she murmured to herself. Fixing Samira's eyes with her hypnotic stare, she started to speak in a peculiar sing song voice.

"I can see difficult times ahead for you. A time of tears and sorrow dearie. But you will overcome all and triumph in the end. You are a strong girl dearie."

Samira started to shift uncomfortably. She tried to get up but the fortune teller held onto her hand.

"You are a strong, strong girl. Your hand shows energy and fortitude. Life gives us sorrows and problems. Only in yourself will you find the strength to overcome them."

Samira was very disappointed with this pronouncement. She snatched her hands out of the fortune teller's grasp and jumped up.

"Come on Rupa. I don't want to hear any more of this."

She stomped off. Rupa smiled at the fortune teller and was about to follow, when the old lady grasped at her hand and stared intently at her palm. Rupa tried to pull her hand away but the fortune teller held on to it, clutching tightly with surprisingly strong fingers.

"Now you, sweet one, will have a hard life also." She rocked slowly backwards and forwards, shaking her head from side to side. Rupa again pulled at her hand.

"Keep still my child. Still!" she commanded staring at Rupa with black glittering eyes. Rupa stood transfixed.

"I can feel a special glow coming from you my child."

The fortune teller closed her eyes and swayed from side to side as if in a trance.

"Your aura is very strong. I am feeling it, it's coming through to me."

Her voice grew fainter, as if she was becoming exhausted.

"You will bring much happiness to many, many people. You are indeed blessed. Blessed by Ganesh," her voice grew stronger. "He is watching over you and always will do."

The watching, mesmerized crowd, broke their silence and murmured in appreciation, smiling at Rupa.

The fortune teller reached into the many folds of her garments and pulled out a little statuette of the elephant god Ganesh.

"Take this!"

Squeezing Rupa's hand hard, she folded Rupa's fingers over the statuette, then turned away.

Rupa frowned at her questioningly but the fortune teller had finished with her, had turned aside and was listening to someone else.

Holding the little statuette Rupa ran after and eventually caught up with Samira.

"I didn't like her. She was rubbish," said Samira petulantly.

Rupa didn't show her the statuette, she pushed it down deep into her pocket.

"What did she say to you Rupa?"

"Oh! Nothing much." Rupa looked away and felt the little statuette hard against her fingers.

"Now go and get the rats Rupa and I'll get the stick and torch."

Samira marched bossily off, the fortune teller forgotten.

4

The Rat-Catcher's Revenge

Three hours later an exhausted Samira and Rupa, with two sacks of dead rats, were banging on the door of the rat-catcher shack.

No reply. There was a sound of singing and loud laughter coming from inside. Samira hammered on the door again.

"He's drunk!" exclaimed Rupa, her eyes opening wide in alarm.

"He'd better not be," muttered Samira.

"He is drunk," repeated Rupa, her ear to the door and a horrified expression on her face.

Samira snatched the long stick from Rupa and thumped the door with it. The singing abruptly stopped. Loud voices were heard from inside. Eventually the door was slowly opened by a dishevelled, scruffy man brandishing a bottle.

"Ah!" he drawled eyeing the sacks. "Wicked! My little helpers plus the booty."

He burst into a drunken song,

"Ratty Tatters, here they are," he warbled, hanging onto the door frame.

"Behold, sweet Ratty Tatters with their bounteous gifts."
He smirked to himself at his 'melodic' serenade.

Samira glared at him and stamped her foot.

"Never mind the Ratty Tatters, we want paying. Thirty
rats we've got, so give us our money."

"Can't do it," the rat-catcher drawled at them soppily.
He turned to laugh at his three friends lying on the floor
drinking bottles of hooch.

"Can't do it," he repeated in a drunken drawling voice,
"spent all my money on..." He held up the empty bottle and
focused his bleary eyes on it.

"Spent it all on.....," a long hesitation followed and a rueful
shake of the head, "on magic tea!"

His friends guffawed at the word 'tea' and rolled about
the floor in hysterics. The rat-catcher slid down the door
and sat, staring gloomily at his bottle.

Samira looked at him in disbelief. "You're drunk! Dead
drunk!" she yelled.

"Too right", he mumbled, "drunk on magic tea."

"Right! You're coming with us to the supervisors office.
You get the money, then you can pay us."

"OK! OK!," he gazed sadly at his bottle. "Ok, I'm coming.
Need some more dosh for tea," he muttered to himself.

Unsteadily, he heaved himself upright giggling and
blinking at Samira.

"Well lady, lead the way!"

He picked up the sacks. Their heaviness nearly caused
him to sit down again. Staggering under the weight of

the sacks, the rat-catcher followed the determined Samira. Keeping a safe distance between herself and the stumbling figure in front, Rupa bought up the rear.

The yard, where rats were counted, was on the main road into the city. Rupa avoided the curious looks from people, as the strange little procession veered in and out of the crowds.

At last they arrived at the yard. The two girls followed the rat-catcher into the room where the rats were counted. Their thirty rats were counted out and removed to a large container. The rat-catcher turned to a stern official, seated behind a desk, to receive his money.

The official looked in disgust at the rat-catcher. He stared long and hard at the drunken shuffling figure before him. Then, turning his hard, gimlet eyes, on an increasingly scared Samira and Rupa, he whispered menacingly,

"And, who are these two?"

The rat-catcher swayed about. Samira grabbed him to hold him steady. The rat-catcher seemed to have difficulty in remembering who they were.

Squinting at the girls, as if he'd never seen them before he eventually bumbled out, "My sisters."

He waved his arm at them, "My dear little sisters."

"Sisters!!" shouted the official banging his desk with his fist, "Who do you think you are kidding? You've been using them to catch the rats."

He opened a drawer in his desk and rummaged about in it. Bringing out a tin, he opened it and took out some notes. Flinging them on the desk he snarled,

"You're sacked! You've been warned enough. You're sacked from this job, this minute. Understand!"

The rat-catcher stared at him open mouthed,

"You can't sack me,"

"Want a bet?" asked the official nastily. "Now get out. No more rats or money for you, you drunken wastrel."

The rat-catcher suddenly seemed to realize that he'd lost his job and his income. Miraculously quickly, he sobered up and fell on his knees.

"Please! Please!" he moaned pathetically. "One last chance."

The official folded his arms and leaned back in his chair.

"No more chances," he spat out. "Take your dear little sisters and clear off."

"You can't do this to me. Please!"

The rat-catcher held out his hands and made a grovelling, stumbling movement towards the official. Whereupon, two big men, who'd been silently watching this little scene, moved threateningly towards him.

Whereupon the rat-catcher suddenly sprang into life. Leaping at Samira, he snatched the long stick from her. Racing to the container, he tipped all the rats onto the floor.

"Gilli danda!" he screamed out. "Gilli danda!" *(Children's game played with two sticks)*

Throwing a rat in the air by its tail, he dealt it a mighty blow with the stick. It flew straight at the official. Splat! It hit him in the chest. A disgusting red stain spread down his immaculate shirt front.

"Urgh!" shrieked the official and fell off his chair.

"Gilli danda!" screamed the rat-catcher again, as he bent down and threw the stinking rat corpses up in the air.

Whacking them in all directions, they were splodged onto walls and smacked up at the ceiling. They sailed gaily into the yard through an open door. People, who were eagerly arriving to witness the bedlam, squealed in fright, ducked their heads and ran for cover.

Crack! And crack again!

They splattered, slopped and dangled on the plastic fans, on tops of cupboards and on the windows. Then leaving ghastly marks, they slid or flopped down to the floor.

Samira and Rupa, who had taken refuge behind a wooden screen, peeped out and watched in horror, the unfolding events.

The two big men attempted to creep up on the rat-catcher, but he spotted them and sent two huge rats flying in their direction. They nimbly dodged them and splat again, the rats landed on the unfortunate official.

The rat catcher now seemed to go completely crazy. All the rats had been lethally despatched and he was totally out of ammunition. So, brandishing the stick above his head, he whirled it round and round. Then, he whirled round and round with it. He had almost succeeded in levitating himself off the ground, when uttering a terrifying scream he launched himself at the official. The official, eyes popping out, gave a strangulated yell and slid down under his desk.

Then catastrophe! The rat-catcher slipped on a squashed rat carcase and fell flat. The two big men seized their chance and jumped on him.

Heaving himself up from under the desk the shaking official jabbed at his phone.

Samira and Rupa clutched each other and watched as the wretched rat-catcher was pummelled mercilessly by his captors. The maddened official took his revenge by joining in.

The sound of police sirens outside alerted the girls to the possibility of trouble for them.

"Let's scram," yelled Samira to Rupa.

With a last look at the prone, seemingly unconscious figure of the doomed rat-catcher, the two girls scarpered. They panted down the big road and didn't stop until they were back in their lane.

Samira was furious.

"Stupid man! Drunken fool! He'll be arrested and we'll not get our money." She stared fixedly at the ground and kicked a stone.

"All that work for nothing. We'll never see him again."

"Good riddance," said Rupa. She stared at her friend's angry face and thought for a moment.

"But he was good at playing Gilli danda wasn't he Samira?"

The two girls looked seriously at each other, then burst out laughing. Holding their stomachs, they shrieked, held onto each other and fell down in a tumbled hilarious heap.

5

Samira Goes Away

Next day Samira didn't meet up with Rupa. Rupa did her usual work, fetching water, running errands, sweeping workshops and carrying tea. She looked anxiously round for Samira, but Samira didn't appear.

Later in the afternoon a worried Rupa decided to hang round Samira's shack to see if she could see her.

The small, round, snotty brother was sitting in the dirt by the shack tormenting a scrawny puppy. It kept trying to escape, but Baljit squeezed its leg tightly with his fat, little hand. The puppy whined, turned its head from side to side and pulled desperately to free itself.

"Where's Samira?" asked Rupa, looking down in distaste at Baljit's dirty face and the mangy puppy.

"She's in there," mumbled Baljit, hanging his head and avoiding looking at Rupa,

"Tell her I want to see her Baljit."

Baljit grabbed the puppy's tail. It frantically turned round and tried to nip him. He then scooped it up and crushed it to his tummy.

Snivelling, he moaned, "Going away. You can't see her Rupa 'coz she's going away."

The puppy whimpered and twisted and wriggled.

"Going away? Where to?"

Baljit wiped his nose with his free hand, then squashed the puppy even closed.

"She's going to work for the rich people Rupa."

"Who said?"

"Dada said."

His bottom lip stuck out and big tears ran down his face as he looked sadly up at Rupa.

"She's got a new dress," he patted the puppy and frowned, "and she's going in a taxi."

"A taxi?"

"Yes. My Dada says she's going to get lots of rupees."

Baljit screwed his eyes shut, opened his mouth and started to wail.

"Don't want her to go away Rupa. Rupa, you make her stay. Tell her Rupa. Tell her!"

His wails got louder and louder. The shack door opened and Samira came out. Not the Samira Rupa knew. She was wearing a clean dress with a long sparkly scarf around her neck. Her hair had been washed and made to lie flat. She had a ribbon tied in it.

Rupa stared at her. Samira kept her head down and her eyes downcast. Samira's Dad came out after her. He was tall and skinny with an irritable look on his face. His shirt flopped over his dhoty and his greasy hair hung down to his collar. He glared at his bawling son.

"Stop that Baljit! Get up and leave that animal alone."

Baljit, on hearing his Father's irritated voice, immediately stopped his bawling. Hiccuping and heaving big shuddering sighs, he reluctantly let go of the puppy. It raced off whimpering and dragging one of its legs. Baljit watched it go, his fingers in his mouth and his nose dripping.

Samira looked up, saw Rupa and quickly looked down again. Rupa made a move towards her.

"Samira?"

A beep sounded from the end of the lane. Samira's Dad gripped her arm and hurried towards the taxi. Rupa reached for Baljit's sticky hand, hauled him to his feet and ran after them.

They both stood and watched as Samira was bundled into the taxi and the door was slammed. Samira's Dad spoke to the driver and the taxi, slowly, was driven away.

A sad face turned and looked out of the back window. A hand gave a little wave. The taxi disappeared into the distance.

"Samira! Where's you going?" yelled a distraught Baljit.

Waiting for a while, he continued sadly, "When's you coming back Samira?"

He then, threw himself down on his fat tummy and punching his fists into the ground, howled at the top of his voice.

His Dad strode over to him, yanked him up and hauled him back to their shack. Baljit's heels dragged in the dust, leaving a long wriggly track behind him.

Silently, Rupa followed. Samira's Mum was peeping anxiously out of her doorway. Her scarf covered her head and she pulled it, with a trembling hand, across her mouth. She quickly withdrew into the shack when she saw her husband. He shoved Baljit inside and shut the door.

"Mama, I'll miss her. She was my best friend. Where's she gone? Baljit couldn't stop crying and her Mother was upset as well."

Rupa and her Mum had finished their evening meal and were sitting quietly in their shack. Rupa's eyes filled with tears. Her Mother was silent for a few minutes. She moved over to Rupa and sat close to her. Gently taking her hand, she said,

"She may have some work Rupa and Samira may be fine."

She paused, as if she found the next bit difficult to say,

"All I know is that some girls are sent away to work. They send money back to their families and then it stops. Sometimes the girls are never seen again."

She looked at Rupa's worried face and continued hurriedly,

"But perhaps Samira will be ok. She could be working for a good, kind family . She can look out for herself, she's a big strong girl."

"But she was worried Mum. She was worried when she saw Mr Chopra's daughters."

"Now listen to me Rupa," Rupa's Mum put both hands round her daughter's face, squashing her thin cheeks and hugging her tight, "as I said, Samira may be lucky."

Rupa bit her lip and silently sobbed. Her Mother thought for a minute and then suddenly smiled,

"How about coming to work with me Rupa? How would you feel about that?"

Blinking away her tears, Rupa jumped up excitedly.

"Mum, that's so wonderful. I can help you. I'll work very hard."

"Well to begin with, you must keep very, very quiet and we'll sort out something for you to do."

Rupa, suddenly stopped leaping about, "But what about my jobs here? Who's going to carry the water?"

"I'm sure you can sort out something," her Mother said reassuringly. "Ask one of your friends. They'll be very glad of the money."

With a big grin at her Mum, Rupa raced outside and up towards Mr Chopra's tea-shop.

The big boys were engrossed in another marble game. They stood in a tight, tense group staring at the ground, whilst one of them squatted down and took aim with his marble. He missed striking a smaller marble and the group hooted in derision. Another boy took his place and the group again, leaned forward in rigid concentration.

Rupa spotted the gang of marble players. Keeping close to the shacks, she slipped past them unnoticed.

Further up the lane a mob of barefooted kids were playing with hoops. Chicken like, they chased about, haphazardly falling over each other and shrieking in high pitched voices. They batted, old bicycle tyres, metal bands from barrels and plastic piping, hacked and joined round into a circle.

The hoops flew up and down chased by the hordes of excited children.

Yelling in delight, they tried to knock each other's hoop over or whacked someone else's further up the lane.

Rupa dodged several whirling circles of plastic and pulled at the arm of a small, scruffy girl attempting to bowl a wonky bicycle tyre.

"Manjit!"

Manjit turned and squinted up at her.

"Rupa!" she exclaimed delightedly. "Have you come to play?" and "Where's your hoop?" she added on noticing Rupa hadn't got one.

"I'm not playing." Rupa shook her head. "Manjit, do you want my water carrying job? Ive got five places I fetch for and I can't do it anymore."

Manjit's face broke into a wide grin, "Oh yes please Rupa. Is it for Mrs Sharma, Mrs Malik, Mrs Mehta, Mrs Khan and Mrs Pal?"

"Yes! How do you know?" Rupa looked curiously at Manjit's delighted face.

"I've seen you Rupa. I've seen you carrying water to them every day."

"Well then, you know where they live and who they are, so, can you start tomorrow? They'll pay you well."

"No problem Rupa and thanks, but didn't Samira want the job?"

Rupa turned away. Manjit looked curiously after her, then with a big push sent her tyre hoop bowling off. It created a wobbly arc, as it bounced down the lane. Manjit chased after it, followed by a pack of small boys. Baljit was at the front, his fat little legs propelling him along. His friends whooped after hims.

Rupa stared at Baljit. Slowly and thoughtfully she walked back home.

6

The Big House

The bus to the big city was so full. Faces pressed against the bars of the open windows. People were standing, squashed tightly together. There appeared to be no room for any more passengers. But, the bus had stopped and the waiting queue surged forward. Thinking that they would never squeeze on, Rupa surged with them. Her Mother grabbed at a hand rail and they balanced precariously on the steps of the bus.

Each time people got off, Rupa thought she'd be swept off with them. Her Mother pressed into her shielding her from the worst of the pushing and shoving.

Earlier that morning, as it grew light, Rupa had rummaged round to find a clean frock. She then went outside and washed her face and splashed her hair with the water from the bucket. Yanking a comb through her hair, she pulled an agonised face at all the knots and tangles she encountered. She then sat back down on her mat and gently tapped her Mother who was still asleep.

"Mother, Mother, I'm ready," she whispered.

Her Mother turned over, opened her eyes and smiled, "Well you're an eager one. Get a chapatti, plait your hair and I'll soon be ready."

So now they were on the bus and Rupa was so excited she could scarcely breathe. What would the big house be like? She had difficulty in imagining it. Hazy pictures of tall towers, pointed windows and strange scented flowers, floated round her mind. Rupa grinned secretly to herself, her nose pressed into the metal side of the bus.

A hand pushed impatiently at her Mother's shoulder. Her Mother felt in her bag and handed some coins to the conductor.

They scrambled off the bus in the middle of the huge, blaring city. Rupa had never seen or heard so much traffic. Buses, taxis, cars, motorbikes and hundreds of pulled rickshaws all whirled past. Honking, beeping, skidding and swerving, they stopped, to let people alight, then continued in the mad, chaotic race again. Where were they all going? Rupa gaped, fascinated at the pandemonium.

In the midst of all this bedlam, two stately cows wandered unconcernedly along. An astonished Rupa glimpsed another, unperturbed cow, sitting down in the middle of the frantic vehicles. She pulled at her Mother's arm and pointed.

Ignoring her, Rupa's Mother hurried towards an imposing wooden door, set in a high stone wall. Stretching on tip toes, she peered through a small window high in the door.

"Mr Biswas!" she shouted through the window, "Mr. Biswas!"

There was a sound of scraping metal and the big door swung open.

Rupa gripped her Mother's skirt as they slipped through. The big door clanged shut behind them.

Immediately, a frantic barking deafened Rupa as two snarling, Alsatian dogs threw themselves at the wires of their large cage. She stiffened in terror as the dogs rebounded off and recharged themselves at the wires, leaping up as if to climb over the top.

"Shut up!!" bellowed a hoarse voice as a huge man emerged from a shack at the side of the Alsatians cage. The dogs instantly cowered down, ceasing their mad leaping's. Growling menacingly, they bared their teeth and gnawed at the wire.

The huge man stood in front of Rupa and her Mother. His mean little eyes squinted down at them. He leered at them, reeking of garlic and bad teeth. An enormous belly hung over his trousers and although he was completely bald, a massive beard and moustache curtained most of his lower face. He's got an upside down face, thought Rupa, quickly suppressing a nervous giggle.

"Who's this then?" he shouted, attempting to be friendly but only succeeding in scaring Rupa witless. Rupa's Mother prised her from her side.

"This is my daughter Mr. Biswas." "Mr. Biswas is the caretaker" she whispered aside to Rupa.

"What's she here for?" He attempted to smile at Rupa. A vision of black teeth and smell of fetid breath caused her to tightly close her eyes. "She's just here to help me Mr. Biswas. She's a very willing child. She won't be in anybody's way."

"Ok! Just keep her out of sight, the family don't like strangers." Losing interest in Rupa and her Mother, he lumbered back into the shack and slammed the door.

The dogs leapt up and started their hysterical barking again. Rupa shivered as she kept her head down and followed her Mother up a wide drive towards a big white house. Pink and white roses, lilies and tall orchids bordered the drive. Gazing timidly round, Rupa breathed in their beautiful scent. A man was digging in the far part of the garden and a boy was helping him. Bees hummed busily round the open blossoms, whilst a small cloud of white butterflies, danced together in the bright morning sunshine. The gleaming house loomed up in front of her. Large windows overlooked green lawns and a curving stairway of stone steps led up to the front door. A veranda, shaded by a stripy canopy ran along one side of the house. On the other side, tall jacaranda trees screened the house from the hot mid-day sun.

Rupa stared. Her mouth hanging open and her eyes wide with amazement. Was this paradise? What kind of people had the blessed, good fortune to live here? Her Mother grasped her hand and propelled her down a small path leading to the back of the house. They descended some narrow steps into a small basement room.

"Sit here Rupa and wait."

Leaving her squatting in a corner, Rupa's Mum disappeared through a door. She reappeared a few minutes later and called to Rupa, "Come on, we're lucky, Mrs. Choudery the housekeeper says she's got some jobs for you."

Rupa got up and timidly followed her Mother.

The door led into a kitchen. It was a large room with two small windows set high up near the ceiling. A large table occupied the centre of the room. Around the walls were cookers, sinks, fridges and cupboards. Rupa stared. She'd never seen so many things crammed in one room. What were they all used for? She stuck her fingers in her mouth and frowned.

Mrs. Choudery laughed when she noticed Rupa's astonishment. Wiping her hands on her overall, she patted Rupa's head.

"Come girl, I'll show you your work" she said in a friendly manner and waddled through the door.

Mrs. Choudery was very fat with a round smiley face and long grey plait down her back. Although she was so fat she nimbly climbed the steps. Rupa followed her.

7

A New Job

Later, when Rupa had been shown the bins, the brushes, the mops and the buckets, she was hard at work.

The bins were outside along the wall at the back of the house. The brushes, mops and buckets were in a store cupboard off the basement room.

Rupa hurried about emptying vegetable peelings into a green bin. Apparently the gardener made them into soil or something. Rupa didn't quite understand this. All the rest of the rubbish, tins, plastic, boxes and wrappings were tipped into three other large bins which the caretaker emptied somewhere. It was all very confusing. The one bin Rupa hated was the left-over food bin. There was a picture of an Alsatian on the front. The dogs ate everything that was tipped out for them.

An outside tap stuck out of the wall by the green bin. Rupa marvelled at it. One tap for one house! But then she remembered seeing other taps in the kitchen and she puzzled over the need for so much water.

Backwards and forwards she went emptying the containers which were dumped in the basement room. Rupa washed out the empty containers using the outside tap. She then left them in the sun to dry. After stacking them all up she carried them back down to the basement room where they were collected by servants who completely ignored her. Not that Rupa minded, she wouldn't have known what to say to them anyway. When Rupa wasn't emptying stuff into the bins and washing out containers, she mopped the steps. After this she picked up a long thin broom and swept the path.

Mrs. Choudery came panting up the steps for some fresh air. She wiped her sweaty face with the back of her hand and sat down heavily on the top step.

"You are a good girl Rupa", she said approvingly watching her sweep the dead leaves. Rupa shyly smiled at her. Mrs. Choudery smiled back, then after closing her eyes for a few minutes, she heaved herself up and returned down to the kitchen.

The sun was high in the sky and the sounds of frantic activity came from below. Pans clanged, plates crashed and voices were raised as the family, who owned the big house, had their mid-day lunch prepared.

Rupa crept down to the bottom step and sat avidly listening to all the noise and trying to make sense of it. Once the kitchen door swung open. She caught sight of her Mum scuttling under the table sweeping up fallen food and peelings. Two young men were waiting by the table for Mrs. Choudery to hand them dishes of steaming food. They then turned round and whisked the food off through a door at the far end of the kitchen. All went quiet as the scurrying feet carried lunch up to the family dining room.

Then pandemonium as empty plates were returned and exchanged for bowls of fruit and sweetmeats.

The bowls were then also returned and Rupa's Mum began the enormous task of cleaning up.

Rupa emptied the buckets of left-over food into the bin with the drawing of a dog on it. She tried to block out the image of the ferocious Alsatians, but couldn't help imagining them leaping out of the bin at her.

The kitchen door clanked and Mrs. Choudery emerged with a plate of rice and vegetables for Rupa. Realising she was very hungry, Rupa squatted down in the shade of the house wall to eat it. The rest of the servants sat together, at the kitchen table to eat theirs.

It was hot, much too hot to work. Mrs. Choudery sat downstairs in a wicker chair, rested her feet on a stool and dozed off. Rupa's Mum started to work on the mountain of washing up and the pile of crusty pans.

Rupa, realising that nothing needed doing for a while, ventured timidly towards the back garden. A large vegetable patch was surrounded by a wide sandy path. Beyond this were shrubs and fruit trees and the surrounding high stone wall.

In the middle of the vegetable patch was a large metal structure with glass windows. Avoiding tripping over the ladders left by the building, Rupa quietly tiptoed up to it and peeped in. The gardener was asleep, lying on some sacks and gently snoring. The boy was asleep, next to him. Surrounding them, on tables and benches were hundreds of plants. Blooms of bright colours, flowers with floaty petals, plants trailing long tendrils, thin plants, bushy plants, plants so tall they reached the ceiling and plants so small that their blossom was like a covering of shiny sequins.

Rupa stared, was this some kind of shop? The gardener gave a groan and stirred in his sleep. Rupa quickly dodged out of sight.

As she turned to return to the house, something caught her attention. Looking up at the tall windows at the back of the house, she saw somebody looking down at her. The person stood very still, half shielded by the window's thin drapes. Rupa screwed up her eyes to see better, then feeling uncertain she abruptly averted her gaze and ran back to the kitchen. Before she got there, she chanced another look. The figure was still there and Rupa saw that it was a young girl about the same age as herself.

8

Aisha

Later in the afternoon the floors had been mopped, the ovens cleaned and the pots and pans put away. Preparations were now beginning for the family's evening meal. The gardener brought in fresh vegetables. Mrs. Choudery laid them out on the kitchen table. Spinach, aubergines, cauliflowers and coriander all awaiting preparing and chopping. Mrs. Choudery called out for Rupa to collect the trimmings.

Rupa, with a bucket, arrived in the kitchen at the same time as the far door swung open revealing a young girl.

"Oh hello Aisha," Mrs. Choudery made a quick bobbing movement, then turned back to the vegetables.

"Who's that?" The girl pointed an imperious finger at a surprised Rupa. Mrs. Choudery paused in her chopping and glanced at Rupa who was twisting the bucket handle and staring at her feet.

"She's Rupa, Aisha and she's come to help." Then by way of an explanation added "Her Mother works here."

"Well I need some help. Can she come with me for a few minutes?"

"I'm not sure your Mother would like a strange child wandering round the house."

"She won't be wandering, she'll be with me."

"Well, just for a short time then."

Mrs. Choudery nodded at Rupa. "Behave Rupa, Aisha is the daughter of the owners of this house."

Aisha beckoned her finger and Rupa with a worried look at Mrs. Choudery, placed her bucket by the wall and followed Aisha out of the kitchen.

Wooden steps led up to a dark passage. At the end a heavy door opened into a large airy room. Long windows and a white marble floor reflected the muted late afternoon light. A huge shimmering glass chandelier dominated the centre of the ceiling. Rupa was terrified. She was a trespasser in an unknown world. She froze still and couldn't move.

Aisha abruptly reached out to her and gripping her hand, pulled her stumblingly up a wide staircase, along a tiled landing and into a room at the far end.

Dropping Rupa's hand she stood directly in front of her and stared unblinkingly at her. Lifting her head, Rupa stared timeously back.

She saw a girl, slightly taller than herself with short black hair parted in the middle and held back by two sparkly hairgrips. Light brown eyes in a small elfin face expressed curiosity and superiority. She was dressed in a white blouse and skirt with white socks and white sandals. Rupa thought she'd never seen anyone so clean and pretty.

"You're name is Rupa?"

"Yes" mumbled Rupa, head down.

Well mine is Aisha. I'm ten and this is my room. It has its own bathroom. Do you have a room Rupa?"

"No"

"I didn't think so."

Aisha slowly scrutinised Rupa from her head to her feet.

"Why are your cloths so dirty and your feet dirty too?"

Poor Rupa looked down at her dusty feet in their dusty flip flops and felt humiliated. Tears threatened to spill down her face.

"I expect you are poor Rupa. That's why you are dirty. Are you poor Rupa?"

Not waiting for an answer she continued intensely, "Would you like to see my special babies?"

Not having the least idea what Aisha was talking about, Rupa nodded.

"Well look then."

Aisha moved from in front of Rupa and waved her arms at her babies.

The dolls were everywhere. In prams, in cots, on chairs and on shelves. Some were standing, some sitting. Some had elaborate curls and some had no hair at all. There were white dolls, brown dolls, boy dolls and girl dolls.

"My babies!" announced Aisha dramatically.

"I have thirty and I am their Mother." She went towards a fat baby doll in a cot and picked it up.

"Sit on my bed Rupa and hold her. She is just like a real baby." Aisha pushed Rupa onto the bed and thrust the baby doll at her.

"I have real baby powder Rupa and bottles. I mix up the formulae and feed them. You can help me Rupa."

Rupa gaped at her and clutched the doll but she didn't have time to think or reply because the bedroom door opened and a tall woman stood there staring in astonishment.

She walked over to the bed and pulled the doll from Rupa. "Who is this dirty, dirty girl and why is she sitting on your clean bed Aisha? Get off! Get off the bed" Rupa quickly slid off the bed. Aisha slyly grinned to herself.

"She followed me from the kitchen Mother," said Aisha, not looking at Rupa, "and she picked up my dolly and sat on the bed. I asked her not to." Rupa shot her a furious look.

"Hmm!" Aisha's Mother seemed to disbelieve this explanation but she pushed Rupa out of the bedroom door saying in a cross voice, "Out you go! Stay down in the kitchen, understood?"

Rupa nodded miserably and with Aisha looking disdainfully at her, she ran along the landing, down the stairs and back to the kitchen. Avoiding Mrs. Choudery's enquiring eyes, she picked up the brimming bucket and went to empty it.

9

Best of Friends

Five days had gone by since Rupa's encounter with Aisha. She hoped that she wouldn't meet her again, ever. She loved her work in the kitchen. Mrs. Choudery continued to be pleased with her and paid her Mother some extra rupees. Rupa had become more confident. She smiled at the gardener and said hello to the many servants. The only person she disliked was Mr. Biswas. He scared her. She avoided looking at him and held tightly onto her Mother's hand when he spoke to her. After a while he stopped attempting to chat and ignored her completely.

Sitting in the shade against the wall after her lunch, Rupa's eyes rested on all the lovely things in the garden. How was it that some people lived here and lots of people were crammed into poor shacks? Rupa frowned and pondered on this but couldn't come up with an explanation. It's just that some people are rich and some are poor, she said to herself. Anyway I'm glad I can work here and not have to carry buckets of water for people. And stand for ages in a queue, she remembered with a grimace. She wondered how Manjit was coping.

The bees buzzed towards the heavily scented flowers and the butterflies again danced among the aromatic shrubs. Rupa's eyelids drooped.

Light footsteps interrupted her dreaming. A shadow moved across her. Aisha was standing directly in front of her. Leaping to her feet Rupa pushed her aside and rushed towards the kitchen steps. She was halfway down when she heard Aisha's pleading voice.

"Come back Rupa. Please come back."

As Rupa turned to look, to her great astonishment Aisha slid down by the wall and sat on the ground. Wrapping her arms round her knees, Aisha stared straight in front of her and said in a small voice, "I've come to say Rupa" Aisha stopped, coughed, then started again. "I've come to say Rupa," she repeated "that I'm very very sorry, I'm ashamed of my mean behaviour towards you." Rupa took a few steps towards her. Aisha turned to look at Rupa and held out her hand, "I mean it Rupa. I'm very sorry. Please say you'll forgive me for lying about you and say that we can be friends?" Rupa didn't say anything. "Please Rupa." Aisha looked near to tears, "I haven't any friends and I'm going away to school soon." She burst into sobs. Rupa slowly sat down next to her and put her arm round Aisha's shoulders.

"Your dress is getting all dusty" whispered Rupa.

Aisha managed a faint grin, "It will be same as yours then!"

Taking one of Aisha's soft brown hands in her strong hard one, Rupa thought for a moment then said, "We can be friends Aisha. Yes we can. I can show you how to be a good friend. I've had lots."

For a second she remembered Samira and sadness overwhelmed her. She blinked back a sudden rush of tears.

From then onwards, after lunch, Aisha would come down to the kitchen to fetch Rupa to play for a few hours. If her Mother knew about it she never said anything and she didn't appear again in her daughter's bedroom. Mrs. Choudery approved. "Do her good," she said to Rupa's Mum "The child is going away to school soon and needs some time to play with a friend."

Rupa adored playing with Aisha. The dolls needed a lot of attention. Dressing, undressing, feeding, washing, putting to bed and waking up. On and on went the routines. Aisha taught her how to mix the formulae and how to pin the nappies. It was wonderful make believe and Rupa never tired of it.

"I've never had a little sister or brother," she said to Aisha one day, as she was dressing a golden haired baby doll.

"I have a brother" replied Aisha, pushing a bottle into a boy doll's mouth. "Well I have two brothers," she continued, "but they are both at university and I don't see them much – there there" she patted the boy doll's back.

"What's university?" Rupa looked puzzled. Aisha laughed "It's where you go to learn complicated things Rupa. Both my brothers are studying to become lawyers. Rupa didn't ask what a lawyer was, she didn't want Aisha to think she was totally ignorant.

"I suppose that's very hard?"

"Yes, it is hard. I want to be a doctor when I grow up and look after poorly babies. What do you want to do Rupa?"

Rupa frowned and couldn't think of anything, but then thought of Mr.Chopra's teashop. "I'd like to have a shop Aisha and sell things, like" she paused lost for ideas. Her eyes fell on the pretty bracelets Aisha was wearing, "Sell things, like bracelets and rings," she blurted out.

Aisha smiled encouragingly, "That sounds fun. Will you make them out of beads and precious jewels?"

Rupa hadn't a clue, so she just nodded her head in agreement. The, feeling rather excited about owning a shop she blurted out "Yes, I'll make them out of jewels and they'll be very expensive and I'll make lots of money." Aisha laughed, "I'll come and buy them Rupa because I'll be a famous doctor." They grinned at each other and nursed the baby dolls.

10

Bad News

That evening, back in their shack, Rupa's Mum looked tired and worried. She had been silent all the way home and Rupa could sense that something was troubling her.

"What's the matter Mum?" Rupa's Mum didn't speak for some time. Rupa waited anxiously. "The big house is being shut up." She said at last.

"Shut up?" Rupa looked at her Mum in alarm.

"Yes, Mrs. Choudery told me today that Aisha is going to boarding school and the two boys are away, so Aisha's Mum and Dad are going to Saudi Arabia for a time.

"Why?"

"Something to do with Aisha's Father's work, computers, Mrs. Choudery said, though I'm sure I don't know what sort of job that will be."

Rupa was shocked.

"What will we do?"

"Well, Mrs. Choudery is going to work in a big hotel. She knows one of the cooks there. She said she'll try and get me some work."

"Mr. Biswas?"

"He's staying and so is the gardener. They will take care of the house. All the other servants have got to leave." Rupa's Mum frowned and avoided looking at Rupa's anxious face.

"We can't stay here Rupa. We'll have to go somewhere. I won't be able to pay the rent."

Rupa held her breath, her big eyes staring fixedly at the floor. Rupa's Mum nervously bit her lip. "Mrs. Choudery knows somewhere near the hotel where we can camp."

"Camp!!?" Rupa's face was one of alarm and disbelief.

"She says that some families have made shelters by the church. St. Andrews, I think its called. Her friend lives there and she'll help us find a space."

Rupa's Mum closed her eyes and pressed her hands over her mouth.

"I don't want to go," Rupa wailed "I'll have no job."

Rupa's Mum opened her eyes and gazed into space. "We've got to go, but not for a few weeks yet."

"A few weeks?"

"Yes a few weeks. When Aisha leaves for school, her parents will leave too"

Rupa was devastated. She curled up on her mat and although she tried not to cry, she began to sob. Her Mother's hand reached out to her and stroked her heaving shoulders. With eyes tightly shut, Rupa reached into her pocket and clutched the little elephant statuette. She thrust it at her Mother.

"Take this! I don't want it. It's fake, it's no good and it hasn't brought me any luck!" Rupa's mum looked at the tear stained face of her child and closed her hand tightly round Ganesh the elephant God. She stroked Rupa's hair.

Two weeks following the bad news, Rupa was walking down the big house's path to the gate with her Mum.

The last two weeks had been so depressing. All the servants were upset and Aisha had cried and cried and said that she would never find another friend like Rupa. Rupa had tried to console her but then she became tearful too. Their tears had fallen on the dolls and they looked as if they were crying in sympathy. It was all very sad and Rupa felt miserable as she clutched her Mother's hand. They reached the large gate.

Mr. Biswas, snoring and dozing in a chair by his front door, woke suddenly and heaved himself up to open the small door in the gate.

Before he opened it he stood in front of them barring their way. Leering down them, he breathed his foul breath in their faces.

"Ganesh is having his outing," he spat at them.

Rupa quickly took a step back as did her Mother.

"Good luck for some, bad luck for others. Look at those crowds."

He flung the door open. Across the road there were hundreds of people surging round the brightly illuminated temple. It was the festival time for Lord Ganesh. The night sky erupted in showers of exploding fireworks.

"Now you two have the bad luck," he continued, grinning at them, "lost your jobs eh!?" he snickered to himself. "I've kept mine. See, some are more lucky than others. Lord Ganesh must like me."

He rubbed his fat belly with a hairy hand.

Rupa frowned and peered up at him. Squinty little eyes, black nostrils, a fat wobbly bristly chin and a gaping toothless mouth confronted her. She gave a gasp of horror and dodged under his arm, pulling her Mum after her.

11

The Miraculous Find

A huge golden statue of Ganesh, the elephant God was outside the temple. Hundreds of men were attempting to move the cart that Ganesh serenely sat upon. The smiling Ganesh was painted all over in a lowing yellow paint. Jewels dangled from his ears and from his decorated trunk. His tusks were adorned with elaborate silver points. Orange, marigold and jasmine garlands hung round his neck. One hand was held up as if to bestow good luck upon the crowd. He seemed to be enjoying the riotous scene before him.

The crowd roared in delight. Some clutched their own statues of Ganesh. Priests wafted scented smoke from their burning lanterns over the people. The men heaved and pulled. Ganesh wobbled on his decorated cart and began to trundle down the road. Fireworks once more lit up the dark sky. The people danced and clapped and followed a much beloved, beaming elephant God. Ganesh, the bringer of good fortune and good luck. Drummers drummed, pipers piped and fire-crackers hissed and popped.

Shrieking and laughing, the children held hands, skipping and hopping with excitement. Ganesh's fat round belly seemed to shake with delight as he was borne down the road towards the sea amidst a river of light and deafening, joyous noise.

"I've got a little Ganesh, somebody gave it to me" whispered Rupa's Mum. Rupa smiled uncertainly at her. "But," she continued, "I've got the best daughter in the world, so I've got all the good luck I'll ever want."

Rupa linked her arm through her Mother's and held her tight.

The bus station was packed with excited people, all intent on celebrating Ganesh's festival. A small boy with no legs was wriggling amongst the crowds, spinning and twirling and delighting in the rupees thrown at him. Men in groups were waving their arms and gyrating to loud music blaring from the station's loudspeakers.

Squeezing and pushing, Rupa and her Mum reached their bus. It was so crowded. With her Mum in front, Rupa managed to get one foot on the bottom step. She grimly hung onto the side rail as the honking bus eased its way through the frenzied scene. Her Mother looked anxiously back at Rupa as she was elbowed up the bus and jammed in along the seats.

The bus gathered speed and swing around a corner. Rupa's foot slipped. She almost let go of the side rail and fell forwards. Then completely losing her grip on the rail she lurched sideways and tumbled off the bus into the road.

Rickshaws honked, taxis swerved round her, people yelled. The bus carried on going and disappeared into the distance. Many hands lifted Rupa and dumped her onto the pavement. Concerned faces stared down at her. Rupa pushed herself up and tentatively felt a big lump at the side of her head. She screwed up her face with pain and moaned softly.

Two young men lifted her to her feet and stood her by the wall of a shuttered shop. "You ok?"

Rupa grimaced but managed to mutter, "Yes thanks. What happened?"

"You fell off the bus"

"My Mother!" Rupa held back her tears, "she was on the bus and now it's gone."

"Have you any money to catch another?"

Rupa felt dizzy but groped about in her pockets.

"No, I haven't. I've not got anything!" She wiped her eyes with the back of her sleeve. The two young men, looked at each other, fished in their pockets and found some coins. "Here have these." Rupa took them gratefully. Seeing that she seemed alright and anxious to join in Ganesh's revelries, the young men left her.

Rupa looked round in bewilderment. Where was the bus station? It couldn't be far. Was this the way? Staggering a little Rupa limped off. She walked for some time but couldn't see the bus station. On reaching a side alley, Rupa paused to catch her breath and rub at her aching head. Although the alley was in total darkness, at the far end was framed an illuminated building. The Temple! It was Ganesh's Temple and the big house was opposite it. She would go back to the big house and Mrs. Choudery would sort things out.

She entered the dark alley, feeling slightly scared, but keeping her eyes on the brightly lit temple at the end. Half way along she came to an abrupt halt as her ears caught the sound of a small whimper. Rats! Oh Mother was it the rats? Rupa's head went dizzy again. She was going to faint. She leaned to the side and felt for the wall.

No, it didn't sound like a rat, nor a dog, more like a kitten's meow. Rupa bent down and with hands outstretched, moved with tiny footsteps towards the direction the small noise. "A kitten, it's a hurt kitten," she whispered to herself.

She almost stood on it. Her foot caught the side of a bundle of dirty cloth. Rupa lifted it up. Holding it close to her face, Rlupa slowly pulled away at the rags, one by one. She uncovered, not a mewling kitten, but a mewling baby. A very small baby, with its fists in its mouth, and whimpering piteously. She almost dropped it in horror. Who had left a baby in this filthy place? Clutching the baby tightly to her, she stumbled to the end of the alley. The joyous crowds took no notice of a bewildered young girl holding a parcel of rags.

It took Rupa a few minutes to hobble to the big house and bang frantically at the door.

Eventually an irritable Mr. Biswas opened the small door "What do you want?" he began, before his mouth lolled open as he was confronted by a dazed Rupa holding a squalling baby. Behind him, the dogs set up a frenzied barking.

"Mrs. Choudery, I need Mrs. Choudery." Pushing past Mr. Biswas, Rupa ran up the path to the big house.

Mrs. Choudery turned in alarm as Rupa burst through the kitchen door. She was talking to the lady of the house, Aisha's Mother. They both gave cries of dismay when they saw what Rupa was clutching. Mr. Biswas, following Rupa, panted down the steps and fell into the kitchen. He pulled himself upright and sat down heavily on a chair.

The two women stared down at the baby. It was now fast asleep with its tiny fists pushed into its mouth. "Oh Rupa! Where did you find the poor thing?" Mrs. Choudery was all motherly concern.

"In an alley Mrs. Choudery. I had fallen off the bus and was coming back here."

"Fallen off the bus?" Mrs. Choudery was confused but she looked tenderly down at the little sleeping face.

"Poor little thing. What are we going to do with you?"

Aisha's Mother abruptly replied "Do with it? it's been abandoned. Thrown away. It will have to go to the orphanage."

Mrs. Choudery frowned and looked disapprovingly at Aisha's Mum. Rupa clutched the bundle more tightly.

Seizing his opportunity Mr. Biswas lunged forward and interrupted. "Pardon me Mrs. Rai, but my wife knows about babies. We can look after it tonight and take it to the orphanage tomorrow."

He attempted an ingratiating smile, but it only succeeded in turning into a leering mask.

Rupa gave a frightened gasp. An orphanage! She couldn't think of a worst fate for a baby and tonight to be in the care of Mr. Biswas's wife. What sort of wife would Mr. Biswas have? Rupa shuddered at the thought of it.

"That's a very good idea Mr. Biswas. You take the child and see that it gets taken to the orphanage tomorrow."

Aisha's Mum ignored Mrs. Choudery's and Rupa's distressed faces. She took the baby out of Rupa's arms and with an expression of distaste, handed it to Mr. Biswas. "It smells! Put some clean clothes on it."

Mr. Miswas, with a muttered "Yes 'm," hurriedly disappeared up the kitchen steps with the pathetic bundle. Crossly, Aisha's Mum turned to a crying Rupa and a protesting Mrs. Choudery "Come come, you can't look after it Mrs. Choudery, you have your duties here. The orphanage will take it, that's what they're there for." She turned to Rupa, "Now you get home Rupa. Babies are no concern of yours. Mrs. Choudery give her some rupees for her bus fare." She gave Rupa a push, "Go on! Your Mother will be worried."

Rupa, with a pleading look at Mrs. Choudery took the coins. Mrs. Choudery shook her head sadly and wiped her eyes with the corner of her apron. Rupa went slowly back up the kitchen steps. Tears ran down her face, she wiped them away with the back of her hand

"Rupa!!!" a slim figure ran across the dark green garden "Rupa! What are you doing back here?" without waiting for an answer Aisha continued excitedly, "Look at the fireworks!" I've climbed a ladder and looked over the wall. Lord Ganesh is being carried down to the sea."

She laughed at Rupa, then suddenly became aware of Rupa's distress.

"Rupa, what is the matter?" Rupa had slumped down in the middle of the path and covered her face with her hands.

"Tell me! Tell me! Rupa what is the matter?" Aisha repeated anxiously. She sat down beside her on the path and put her arms round her. She felt Rupa trembling and held her more closely.

"Tell me Rupa. Tell me, your friend."

"I fell off the bus Aisha," Rupa lifted her wet tear streaked face to Aisha's. "I was coming back to your house and I found a baby in a filthy alleyway. It was so little Aisha and it was crying. I brought it back here.." She gulped and bit her lip. "Now Mr. Biswas has got it and it's got to go to an orphanage." She burst out crying again.

Aisha stared at her. Her face expressed total amazement, bewilderment and then deep concern.

12

Rescue

M r. Biswas? A live baby?"
"Yes your Mother gave it to him." Rupa wailed.
"My Mother gave it to him? Gave it to Mr. Biswas?"
"Yes Aisha and now he's looking after it. Him and his wife."
Poor Rupa rocked backwards and forwards in agony. Then
blurted out between sobs, "He's taking it to the orphanage
tomorrow." A shower of rockets roared up into the black sky.

Aisha sat back on her heels, frowning and staring at the
bright fireworks. Then, seemingly galvanized by the rockets
energy, she jumped to her feet pulling Rupa up with her.

"We'll see about that!" she muttered grimly.

"Follow me Rupa."

It was now very dark in the garden. Aisha ran lightly
over the lawns towards the big gate. Rupa seemed alarmed
at Aisha's sudden action, but then she quickly followed.

Mr. Biswas's front door was shut. The dogs leaped to
their feet but when Aisha shushed them, with her fingers
to her lips, they crouched down and wagged their tails.

Tugging Rupa's arm, she stealthily pulled her round
to the back of the shack. The windows were half open and
they both cautiously peeped in.

"Look!" whispered Aisha. The baby was in a cardboard box on the floor of what seemed to be the kitchen. Mr. Biswas and his wife were talking. Their backs were to the windows. The girls strained their ears to hear what they were saying. "You can get a good price for a new baby." Mrs. Biswas, an ugly woman with narrow eyes and a large bent nose, pursed her thin lips and nodded.

"Sanjit knows how to sell them on. I'll take it to Sanjit tomorrow." Mr. Biswas and his wife, without glancing down at the baby, moved out of the room leaving the child in the box on the floor. The sound of a television quiz show came from an upstairs room.

After waiting a few minutes, Aisha sprang into action. "Quick!!"

She heaved at the window and pushed it wide open. She climbed up onto the sill and dropped down into the room. Tip-toeing quickly across the floor she carefully lifted up the cardboard box. Tip-toeing quickly back she lifted it through the window into Rupa's waiting arms. She hurriedly scrambled out after it, catching her foot on the sill and falling head first onto the ground. She lay there winded. Rupa crouched down beside her. Holding their breath, they listened for any raised voices from upstairs. Only the excited noise from the quiz show drifted down to them.

Rupa, clutching the box tightly stood up and reached with her other arm to pull Aisha to her feet. Both girls then fled up the patch, across the lawn and into the big house.

The baby jiggled about in its box. Rupa dreaded it starting to cry. Instead, whilst being rocked about, it opened its big black eyes and unblinkingly stared at her. Rupa tripped and almost dropped the box. Staring back at the baby she felt an instant love overwhelm her.

The two girls scooted up the grand staircase and into Aisha's bedroom. Locking the door, they both fell on the floor shaking uncontrollably.

Aisha recovered first. She leaned over the cardboard box and gently stroked the baby's downy head.

"A baby! A real live baby Rupa." Pulling herself up, she said determinedly "We've got to hide it Rupa, and think of a plan."

Rupa had touched the baby's hand and was engrossed in feeling the little baby's grip on her fingers.

Aisha looked round her room and grinned to herself. "And what better place to conceal a baby Rupa? Look!"

She waved her arms at all her dolls. To Aisha's eyes, they were all smiling in complete agreement. Rupa excitedly nodded her head. "See," continued Aisha, "we've got clothes, nappies and powdered milk. We've got everything a baby needs." She frowned in concentration, "We're going to look after it for now Rupa. We'll work out some solution later."

She dreamily looked down at the small baby and softly stroked its cheek. "But we don't know what it is" interrupted Rupa. "We don't know whether it's a boy or a girl. Let's find out Aisha," she whispered.

They carefully lifted the little person out from the box and laid it on the floor. Rupa started to undo the rages wound round it. It still continued to sleep, its fists tightly in its mouth. The last rag was unwound.

"It's a girl!" exclaimed Aisha, and she's so sweet. She'll have to have a name Rupa now we know it's a girl."

She thought for several minutes, twining her hair round her fingers. "Amrita, Rupa. Let's call her Amrita. It means nectar. The bees love sweet nectar from the flowers and our little baby is sweetness itself."

"Amrita. Amrita," repeated Rupa. "That's lovely Aisha. We'll call her Amrita."

"Now, put her back in the box Rupa. I'll go and get the formulae and a bottle. It will have to be mixed with cold water but she won't mind that, I hope. You find her some clothes and nappies Rupa. My baby doll's clothes will fit her perfectly and she'll be able to sleep in the big doll's cot."

Aisha dashed into her bathroom for her doll's feeding bottles. She lifted the powdered formulae from off a shelf and read the instructions carefully. After mixing it with bottled water she poured it into a feeding bottle.

Rupa, in the meantime, had found the doll's disposable nappies and had undressed a blonde haired baby doll. Baby Amrita now had a nappy, vest, dress and a cardigan, plus a cot diversed of its previous occupants who were tipped out onto the floor.

"Do we feed her or dress her first?" Rupa looked anxiously at Aisha, then worriedly down at the still sleeping Amrita.

Aisha frowned and thought for a second. "Let's wake her and feed her. She won't then cry when we are dressing her."

"You feed her Aisha. You've had lots of practice with your dolls."

Confidently, Aisha picked up the baby and sitting cross legged on the floor, gently put the teat of the bottle into Amrita's mouth. The baby shook her head, grimaced and spat it out. Milk dribbled down her chin. Aisha gently persisted in pushing the teat back. The baby seemed to resist, but then she relaxed and, still keeping her eyes shut began sucking eagerly at the bottle.

"There, there," crooned Aisha, "Who's a good little girl?"

The girls smiled at each other and Rupa put her arm round Aisha and listened to the baby's soft sucking sounds.

Suddenly there was a sound of raised voices coming from the stair. The girls froze. Rupa leaped up and stared horrified at Aisha and the baby. Aisha quickly reacted.

"Throw the box out of the window Rupa and play with the dolls" she hissed. She then dived into the bathroom with Amrita. Rupa hurriedly picked up the box, opened the window and threw it out, along with the rags Amrita had been wearing. She then flung herself on the floor with several dolls and pretended to play with them, whilst trying to control her violent trembling.

The door burst open and there stood Aisha's furious Mum with Mr. Biswas close behind her.

"Rupa! I thought I told you to go home straight away.

Your Mother's arrived in a state thinking you were missing and Mr. Biswas tells me the baby has also gone missing."

She strode over to Rupa and shook her, "What do you know about this?"

Aisha, coolly stepped out from the bathroom.

"Mother, what is all this fuss about? I invited Rupa up to play for a few minutes." She lifted her eyebrows enquiringly. Mr. Biswas has lost the baby you say? Well perhaps it's been stolen, poor thing."

"Yes! But who stole it?" yelled Mr. Biswas, his eyes bulging in anger.

"Shush!!" commanded Aisha's Mother. "Now Aisha, if you have anything to do with....."

"Look round Mother," interrupted Aisha, "How could a baby be here?"

"Very easily" muttered Mr. Biswas. Aisha glared furiously at him. Aisha's Mother went over to the bathroom and opened the door. She looked carefully around. Rupa held her breath. She then went to Aisha's large wardrobe, unlocked the door and pushed back the clothes. Rupa didn't dare look at Aisha. Mr. Biswas, furtively sneaked a look under the bed and in the doll's cot.

Satisfied that there was no baby in the room, Aisha's Mother turned to Mr. Biswas, who hurriedly left off squeezing all the dolls along the shelves.

"Somebody has taken it, but it's not here. I suggest you look around the grounds for clues. It's not here Mr. Biswas!" She repeated in an exasperated tone.

"Well why didn't the dogs bark?"

"I've no idea. Perhaps the kidnapper was one of your friends. Now I've got visitors to see to. This has taken up too much of my time. Rupa, go down to your Mother right away." She pushed her towards the door. "Aisha, it's your bedtime."

With that she swept out of the room. Mr. Biswas gave Aisha an evil stare which momentarily rested on a patch of dirt on her skirt. Reluctantly he followed her out. Rupa turned to look questioningly at Aisha who touched her lips with a finger and smiled.

13

The Plan

When Aisha was satisfied that everyone had safely departed, she locked her bedroom door and dashed to the bathroom. Lifting up the toilet seat she carefully pulled out the small baby. She stuffed the towels crammed into the toilet into the linen basket.

Cradling the baby in her arms, she softly sang to it. Amrita opened her eyes and gave Aisha her first smile. Aisha hugged the warm little body close to her.

The girls had been hiding the baby for two weeks with no definite idea what to do with her. Aisha wanted to keep her for ever. In the mornings she would put her in a pram and trundle her round the garden. She'd often done this with her dolls so nobody took much notice. She kept well away from everyone especially Mr. Biswas who wasn't allowed in the family areas.

Amrita never cried and she never woke in the night. Aisha was first aware of her waking by the sounds of cooings and gurglings floating round the bedroom. She smiled and smiled and waved her little fists.

Aisha and Rupa were besotted with her. They carefully read all the instructions on the formulae packets, and meticulously rinsed out the bottles and the teats. They spent the afternoons bathing and dressing her, singing her songs and rocking her to sleep.

One morning, however, all the staff were summoned to the large hallway of the big house. The servants stood quietly giving each other anxious looks. They knew what was coming.

Mrs. Rai swept into the room. "I told you some weeks ago that, we were leaving India for a time," she loudly announced "Well", she continued "we shall be leaving next week and Aisha will be boarding in her new school."

All the servants shuffled their feet and stared glumly at the ground.

"You will be given four weeks money on Saturday when I expect you all to depart. Thank you for your services and I wish you well."

She left the hallway without a backward glance at the distressed servants. Mrs. Choudery pulled a gloomy face and glanced at Rupa's Mum. They walked slowly back towards the kitchen with Rupa trailing after them.

"Rupa!" Rupa caught the sound of Aisha's voice. Aisha was signally to her at the top of the stairs. She quickly left her Mum and joined Aisha. Aisha was distraught. "I'm going away to school next week. Next week!" She gulped, trying to control her emotions. Tears spilled down her face.

"What are we going to do with Amrita?"

Rupa pulled Amrita into her bedroom and shut the door.

"Don't worry Aisha. We'll think of something. I can take Amrita and when you finish school you can come and find us."

"Where will I look?" wailed Aisha. "Oh Rupa, I'll never find you and I'll never see Amrita again and I love her so much." She burst into loud sobs.

Rupa moved close to her and held her tightly. "Yes you will Aisha. You'll find us. I'll keep Amrita safe always, I promise you."

"Will you Rupa? Will you keep her very, very safe?" cried Aisha.

"Yes," replied Rupa very seriously. "I'll never let any harm come to her. I promise this to you and Lord Ganesh and to all the other Gods in the world."

Aisha smiled through her tears, "That's an enormous promise Rupa,"

Rupa nodded and hugged Aisha close.

That night Rupa decided to confide in Mother. She waited until they'd had supper and were unrolling their bed mats. "Mother," she began tentatively.

"Shush Rupa, I'm ready to sleep and I've got to think about our plans to move."

"Mother, I've got something very important to talk to you about and it can't wait."

Hearing the seriousness conveyed in Rupa's voice, she sat back on her heels and looked enquiringly at her daughter. "Well go on then," she said encouragingly. Rupa swallowed hard.

"You know the baby that went missing?" Rupa's Mum gave a sharp intake of breath, almost guessing what Rupa was about to say.

"Aisha and I took her."

"What!?" exclaimed her Mother.

"We took her because we didn't want her to go to an orphanage and also because we found out that Mr. Biswas was going to sell her."

"Sell her?"

"Yes! She's a little girl baby and Aisha and I overheard Mr. Biswas talking to his wife about what he was going to do with her."

"So you took her?"

"Yes we did Mum. We rescued her. Aisha is looking after her but now she can't because she's going to school and the house is being closed on Saturday" Rupa's voice broke into a wail.

"Shush darling" Rupa's Mum stroked Rupa's hair. "You two are very brave girls, very very brave. I'm so proud of you both."

"But now you can see, we have a big problem." Rupa bit her bottom lip.

"I can see that" nodded her Mum.

"And I've thought of a solution."

"Does it include me?"

"Yes it does Mum."

"I thought it might"

Rupa took her Mum's hand in hers. "Can you listen to my plan and tell me if you think it will work?"

14

The Escape

On the final Saturday, all the servants lined up to say goodbye to Aisha's family. They then trundled sadly off with their various bundles, bags and cases. Rupa's Mum hugged Mrs. Choudery and promised her that she would move to the shelters by the Church.

"See you Rupa." Mrs. Choudery, looking tearful disappeared down the steps to the kitchen to collect her belongings.

Rupa gave her Mum a quick glance and ran quickly round to the bins. Making sure no one was watching she heaved at the waste food bin. It fell over onto its side and a heap of discarded food scraps rolled out from it. Keeping close to the house wall, Rupa sneaked back up to Aisha's bedroom. Her Mother continued down the path to the gate.

"Where's Rupa?" asked Mr. Biswas suspiciously

"Oh she'll be along" said Rupa's Mum nervously, "She's doing something for Mrs. Choudery."

"She'd better hurry. I'm letting the dogs out."

Rupa's Mum hurried through the gate but instead of making her way towards the bus station, followed the big house wall for some distance. She was looking upwards for something. There it was, the top of a ladder protruding over from the house garden. Sitting down by the wall she waited.

In Aisha's bedroom, Rupa had fashioned a sling out of some long scarves. Aisha looked down at the smiling baby in one of her doll's cots. She lifted her up, nuzzled her face into Amrita's soft warmth, then hurriedly placed her in the sling round Rupa.

"There that's secure. She'll not fall out."

Aisha then looked at Rupa, "Look after her Rupa." She turned her head away and bit her lip.

There was a furious banging at the bedroom door.

"Open the door Aisha!"

"We know you've got her!"

Aisha's Mum and Mr. Biswas were outside the bedroom door.

"Quick! Through the window" Flinging the window open, Aisha briefly touched Amrita as Rupa scrambled through and dropped down on to the ledge of the window below. With a fearful look above her, Rupa leaped down from the window into the flower beds. With Amrita tied safely to her back she scarpered across the lawns.

For a brief moment, Aisha stood by the window. She closed it, pressed her forehead to the glass, and then went to open her bedroom door. Running back to her bed she threw herself onto it and pulled the covers over her head.

The sounds of snarling dogs terrified the fleeing Rupa. But then she remembered the bins. The dogs had found the food and were fighting each other for the best bits. Angry shouts sounded nearer and nearer. The ladder, where was the ladder that Aisha told her she had placed against the wall? The greenhouse loomed in front of her and horror, there was the threatening figure of Mr. Biswas coming round the far side.

Panicking, Rupa dodged into the greenhouse. Mr. Biswas lumbered in after her.

"Got you now!" screamed Mr. Biswas. Rupa realised she was trapped. With her heart pounding, she fled to the back of the greenhouse and crouched down behind some shelves. Holding her breath and feeling faint, she pressed up against the plant pots. Mr. Biswas crept towards her.

"Come out Rupa," he called peering round in the dark.

"Come out Rupa. I know you are hiding and you've got that baby."

Amrita gave a faint squeak and then made a gurgling sound.

"Aah, Haaa!!" roared Mr. Biswas. "I know where you are Rupa!"

Rupa in a blind terror, stood up as Mr. Biswas darted towards her. She pushed at the shelves. They wobbled and several plant pots fell off. A large pot with a bushy, prickly plant in it tipped over. It fell and clouted Mr. Biswas on the head.

He yelled and stumbled about. Rupa blindly waved her arms about and they gave the shelves another almighty shove. Over they went with a deafening crash. Mr. Biswas was felled. He lay flattened under the shelves with the plants and their pots tumbled around him. Soil, roots and strands of greenery covered his face. He let out a muffled howl.

A petrified Rupa ran madly back out of the greenhouse and towards the garden wall.

Amrita, bouncing up and down on her back, let out little squeals as she was shaken from side to side.

Where was the ladder?

Hurriedly, Rupa's eyes flicked from side to side searching for it. At last she spotted something. Was that it? There, behind the tall jacaranda tree? Was that the ladder? Oh blessed Ganesh, make it so.

Rupa rounded the tree and, gasping for breath, gave a quick thank you to Ganesh and hauled herself up the ladder. Peering over the top, she shouted down to a seated figure. Her Mother leaped to her feet and waved.

Lifting her leg up over the top of the wall, Rupa sat astride it and kicked the ladder away. It fell sideways amongst some shrubs.

"Quick Mum! Hold out your arms for Amrita."

Rupa pulled and fumbled at the scarf's knots. Would they ever untie?

A loud bellow came from below her. There stood the menacing figure of Mr. Biswas. A Mr. Biswas in a towering temper. Dirt streaked his face and a dangly leaf poked out from behind his ear.

"Got you!" he screamed and bent down to lift up the ladder. Beneath her trembling fingers, Rupa felt the tight knots give way. Hurriedly she slid her arms out of the sling.

Leaning over as far as she could, she dropped Amrita into the waiting arms of her Mother. For one heart stopping moment, Rupa thought that she might drop her, but her Mother caught her and tightly grasped her.

Holding onto the top of the wall and feeling with her feet for toe holds, Rupa quickly tried to lower herself down.

Then the ladder suddenly swung up beside her. Rupa stared at it transfixed. Two hot sticky hands grabbed at hers. Stifling a horrified scream, Rupa let go of the wall and balanced precariously on a small ledge. Holding her breath she jumped down to the ground and pitched forward onto her knees. Moaning with pain she scrambled up and both she and her Mother scarpered down the road. Mr. Biswas' shouts receded into the distance. Pausing to get her breath, Rupa's Mum peered down at Amrita and placed her hand protectively over the baby's head.

A taxi pulled up nearby and its passenger got out. An ear piercing shriek sounded as Mr. Biswas appeared in view. Rupa's Mum pushed Rupa into the taxi and scrambled in after her. A furious Mr. Biswas was left shaking his fists as the tax sped away.

Back at their home, Rupa's Mum tenderly rocked Amrita.

"She's a lovely baby Rupa. You and Aisha looked after her really well"

Rupa looked down at the smiling Amrita. "It was mainly Aisha, Mum. She knew exactly what to do and she's tucked a bottle and some formulae round Amrita's middle."

"Yes it's here. What a thoughtful girl."

"She wants to be a children's doctor when she gets bigger."

"I think she'll be wonderful. Rupa, can you boil some water on the stove and we'll give Amrita her bottle?"

Rupa boiled the water and mixed some powder into it. She poured it into the bottle and fastened the top back on.

There was a small tap, tap, on the door. Rupa gave the bottle to her Mum and went to open it.

"Samira!"

A confident, tall Samira stood there in front of her. She was dressed in a yellow sari with an orange fringed scarf. Her hair had grown longer and was pulled back off her face and fastened with a large sparkly clip. She grinned at Rupa. "Samira! You look so grown up," gasped Rupa. "How was the job?"

"Ok," shrugged Samira, her grin disappearing. "I left it, but now I have a great job with Mr. Kumar. He's made his café much bigger and does food there. I am in charge of the cooking. I learnt it at the hotel."

"Hotel? I didn't know you were working at a hotel."

"Well it was a sort of hotel."

Samira didn't seem to want to talk about it anymore, so Rupa asked, "How's Mr. Kumar's daughters?"

Samira laughed, "Brilliant! One of them is married and the other is engaged. One lives back at home but I don't see her, she is too busy with wedding plans." Changing the subject she looked down at Amrita.

"And who is this?"

"This is Amrita, Samira. I found her in an alleyway when she was very small. We've just rescued her from this horrible man, Mr. Biswas. He wants to sell her!"

Samira suddenly looked very sad, "Yes that's what sometimes happens to abandoned babies" She heaved a big sigh. "Can I hold her Rupa?" Rupa's Mum smiled and handed Amrita and her bottle to Samira.

Samira looked wistfully at Amrita and carefully held the bottle to Amrita's lips. Amrita sucked away and waved her little fists at Samira.

"I had a... "began Samira, but was rudely interrupted by a violent shouting from outside. The door was pushed open and there stood Mr. Biswas. Who had told him where they lived?

"Give me that baby" he snarled, advancing towards Samira. She took a hurried step backwards.

"Give me that baby. "It's mine"

Rupa and her Mum clutched each other. Samira quickly recovered herself,. She was more than a match for Mr. Biswas.

"Yours?" she whispered ominously, stepping back towards him. "Yours?" she repeated even more quietly

"Yes mine," he snarled again. "Give it to me!"

Samira took a deep breath, she scowled at Mr. Biswas. Then – "How dare you!" she yelled in his face. "This is my baby! Mine!" she repeated. I'll get the police on you, you big fat oaf. Get Out! Move yourself! You, Mr. Biswas are an evil man and you want to abduct my child. That's a very serious offense" Amrita's big eyes fixed unblinkingly on Samira's face but she kept sucking vigorously at her bottle.

By this time, alerted by the noise, a crowd of people had gathered outside. The men pushed in front of the women and crowded into the shack. Mr. Biswas looked at them in alarm. One man pushed up to him angrily.

"Clear off right now baby stealer"

Someone else joined in, "Shove off! Don't you understand what Samira said? Get moving!"

He jostled Mr. Biswas towards the door. Other men joined in. Mr. Biswas was pushed about and a few blows aimed at him. He attempted to resist, but realising he was completely outnumbered, broke free from the men and fled. The crowd followed shouting abuse and hooting in derision.

Samira laughed loudly and reluctantly handed Amrita back to an anxious Rupa. "That sorted him out," she laughed again and hugged Rupa, but then became serious, "I hear you've got to move Rupa."

Tears sprang into Rupa's eyes. "Yes, we have Samira. We can't afford the rent for this place. Mum hasn't got a job. Somebody said we can have a shelter near St. Andrews Church."

Samira looked troubled, "Will you be ok? You won't be troubled by that horrible man anyway."

"Thanks for that Samira" Rupa smiled "You're not afraid of anybody!"

"Only a mad rat-catcher," laughed Samira. She hesitated, before again repeating worriedly, "will you be ok?"

Rupa heaved a sigh, "I hope so Samira, who knows?"

Samira rummaged in a small bag hanging over her shoulder. She took out a small purse.

"I must go now Rupa. I've got to go to work. Take this. It's not much money, but it might help." She handed Rupa the small purse. Rupa took it gratefully.

"Thank you," she whispered. "Well, see you! Take care!"

With a last glance at Amrita, Samira hurried out. Rupa and her Mum started to pack up their belongings.

15

Rupa's Sadness

St. Andrews Church had iron railings round it. Attached to the railing was a row of makeshift shelters.

"Mrs. Choudery said there was one at the end" said Rupa's Mum. She was carrying Amrita on one hip and had rolls of bedding under the other arm. She looked weary and out of breath. Rupa was plodding behind carrying a bag of clothes and a few pots and pans.

They made their way to the slum dwellings. The last one seemed to have collapsed. The plank supports had partly fallen in and black plastic flapped uselessy round them.

"Is this it?" asked an incredulous Rupa. "We can't live here."

"We must. There's nowhere else and it's free."

As if lacking any more energy, Rupa's Mum sat down on the pavement. A woman came out of the next shelter and scrutinised them. "I'm Mrs. Dhaliwall," she said "Are you Mrs Choudery's friends?" Rupa nodded.

"This place is wrecked," she continued, gesturing towards the flapping plastic. "I don't think you can stay here."

Rupa looked at her Mother's depressed figure and said, "We've got to stay here. There's nowhere else for us. I can fix it up. "Can you lend me a hammer and some nails?"

"I'll get some for you."

Mrs. Daliwall disappeared back into her shelter and reappeared carrying several large sheets of plastic and a big hammer. "Come on, I'll give you a hand," she said kindly, glancing with some concern at Rupa's Mum. Rupa's Mum sat staring into space with a look of utter dejectedness on her face. Amrita lay on the pavement smiling and waving her hands at something only she could see.

Rupa held the plank supports whilst Mrs. Daliwall hammered them back into place. When the box like structure seemed stable, they nailed the plastic back in position.

The new sheets of plastic they draped over the top.

"I'll get some long pieces of wood to weight it down," said Mrs. Daliwall. "We don't want it blowing away." From the back of her shack she fetched some long branches. Standing on tip toes she pushed them onto the top of the dwelling.

"There! That'll have to do," she said at last.

"Now over there is a stand pipe where you can get some water and the toilets are at the back of the Church. Will you be ok?" she asked anxiously looking again at Rupa's Mum.

We'll be fine," replied Rupa "and thanks."

Folding back the plastic sheeting she entered her new house.

It was almost unbearable to live in. During the hot summer months they slept outside on the pavement. When the monsoon came the heavy rains leaked into the shack. The wind blew and Rupa was constantly nailing the loose sheets of plastic back in place. Her Mother grew more weary and tired. Increasingly Rupa shouldered the responsibility of Amrita and of feeding the three of them.

When her Mother dragged herself off to clean the hotel where Mrs. Choudery worked, Rupa slung Amrita on her hip and went off to forage for sellable rubbish. Amrita was getting heavy so Rupa couldn't walk very far. Even so, she managed to find some cans and bottles that she sold to a man by the station.

Hundreds of kids lined up to sell their finds. The man weighed the sacks and begrudgingly handed out a few rupees. He bawled and screamed at any kid who protested they hadn't been paid enough.

"Don't come back," he'd yell, pushing them. But of course they did, they had no one else to turn to.

Amrita was now beginning to stagger about on her spindly little legs. Rupa asked Mrs. Dhaliwall if she could look after her for a short time.

"I've got too much to do," said Mrs. Dhaliwall, "but you could leave her at the Church. They have a playgroup for small children some afternoons. Go round and ask them."

Rupa did and Amrita toddled off to play with thirty other small children. She was delighted.

Work became increasingly hard for Rupa. Her Mother appeared more tired as each day passed. She could barely drag herself off to work in the early morning.

One evening, when the monsoon rain was falling heavily, she didn't come home. Rupa waited anxiously for her, peering out at the flooded street and black skies. She then, exhausted by her day's work, fell fitfully asleep hugging Amrita close to her. She woke several times in the night and patted at the thin mattress next to hers. It was empty, nobody was sleeping there.

As dawn broke, Rupa slung a sleeping Amrita onto her hips and rushed to Mrs. Dhaliwall's shack. Mrs. Dhaliwall was about to get a bucket of water from the standpipe.

"Mrs. Dhaliwall! My Mother's not come back and I don't know what to do."

"Not come back!? Oh she's probably slept over at her work. She'll be back later you'll see."

"Do you think so?" Rupa's brow wrinkled in worry. "She's never slept over before."

"She'll be back later." Mrs. Dhaliwall gave a reassuring nod. "Now don't you upset yourself."

All that long day Rupa was beset by troubling thoughts. She finished her foraging and dashed to collect Amrita who could now totter along quite independently. Holding her hand Rupa walked slowly back to the shack. She was filled with a dull sense of foreboding which increased as she approached her home. Still no sign of her Mother. She sat and waited. Amrita sat quietly beside her playing with a broken plastic doll. When she could wait no longer, Rupa sprang to her feet and ran to Mr.s Dhaliwall's. Stumblingly Amrita followed her, the doll abandoned.

Mrs. Dhaliwall listened again to Rupa.

"Go down to the police station by the railway." She told Rupa. "They may know something. I'll look after Amrita."

Rupa set off to trek to the police station. It was back near the place where she sold her bottles and cans. When she eventually arrived the man was still yelling and the kids still waiting in a long line. The police station's door was open and several officers stood outside smoking.

The police officers barely glanced at the poor barefooted girl approaching them. They turned nonchalantly away and puffed on their cigarettes. Timidly Rupa went up to them. One officer flicked his cigarette end away and turned to go back into the police station. Rupa touched his arm. He looked down at her and brushed her hand from off his tunic.

"What do you want?"

"Missing person." Rupa's voice faltered. "How do I find out about a missing person?"

He stared at her for some minutes then said "Come with me."

Rupa followed him as he marched through the police station's doors.

At as large desk sat an official looking elderly man scrutinising a computer.

"Tell him what you want," snapped the officer and left. The elderly man's eyes reluctantly left the computer and fixed themselves irritably on Rupa.

"Well?" he said crossly.

Rupa swallowed nervously, "My Mother is missing."

"For how long?" he snapped back.

"Two days."

The man shrugged impatiently, "Well that's no time! Go away! Come back in a week."

"But she's never been away before," Rupa persisted.

"There's always a first time."

Rupa turned away, but just as she turned she noticed something on the desk. It was a small statuette of Ganesh. Gazing at it in horror she picked it up.

"Where did you get this from?"

"Oh, some old lady got knocked down and that was in her pocket."

"Is she dead?" Rupa could barely get the words out.

"Yes she's dead alright. Stepped off the pavement and got hit by a taxi. Nobody knew who she was, so she's been taken to the mortuary with hundreds of others."

He suddenly stopped talking and stared at her. "Do you think she was your Mother?" He said more gently.

Rupa started to sob and wiped her eyes with the corners of her skirt.

"Yes this is her Ganesh."

"Well keep it then. Your Mother has been taken away. You'll not find her amongst the many dead and her soul has already departed." He patted Rupa's hand "Now go back home to your family."

Family! What family? Rupa stumbled out of the police station and staggered back to the shack. Mrs. Dhaliwall took one look at her and went to fetch Amrita. Amrita lifted up her little arms and Rupa reached down to hug her close. Her tears fell down onto Amrita's curly hair.

16

Amrita Finds
a Friend

The following years were hard for Rupa. She did think of going back to see Samira but where would she stay? Such a long, long time had gone by.

Amrita had become too old for the play group and school was too far away and cost too much. Rupa simply could not afford it. So Amrita spent most of her time playing around the shack and waiting for Rupa to come back. Mrs. Dhaliwall kept an eye on her but most of the time she was left to her own devices. "I want to come with you," she would moan to Rupa.

"No you can't. Not yet. Wait for me, Mrs. Dhaliwall is about. What is the matter with you Amrita?" She continued crossly. "You know I have to earn rupees for us, don't you?" She gave Amrita a quick hug and left with her sack slung over her shoulder.

Amrita sat down outside the shack and watched her big sister stomp off. Rupa turned to wave as she reached the alleyway then disappeared down it.

Mrs. Dhaliwall appeared and looked at the dejected Amrita.

"I'm just off to the store Amrita. Don't go off anywhere. I'll bring you back some jellabees and here, have this samosa. I know you like them."

She handed Amrita a samosa, pulled a scarf over her head and set off towards the church. The stores were at the far side of it. There she met a friend and they decided to have some tea together and a good gossip.

Amrita put the samosa in her pocket. She'd save it until later. Meanwhile she was bored. She went into the shack and tidied it. She folded up the thick blankets and put two plastic beakers into the water bucket. There was nothing much else to do so she wandered outside.

Where was Rupa? Just down the alleyway? She'd have a peep and see if she could see her. I'll meet her at the end of the alleyway, she thought. I'm a big girl now. When Rupa sees me she'll take me with her. I can find things like she does. Whilst she was thinking all this, she was walking down the alleyway towards a very busy street.

There was no sign of Rupa, but there were hundreds of people about. Families were squatting on the pavement selling clothes, cooking food, cajoling the passers-by to look at their jewellery, watches, pens, ornaments, garlands of marigolds etc. Young men drove carts pulled by donkeys, bicycles swerved in and out laden with bales of alfalfa, parcels, carpets and other mysterious packages.

Taxis honked and cows strolled calmly along or lay in the gutter chewing on something they had foraged.

Amrita was bewildered. The crowds pushed her along. She couldn't see where she was going and stumbling she fell off the pavement. Somebody grabbed at her and hauled her back.

"Watch it little girl," breathed a garlicky voice "You'll get run over." The grip on her arm tightened.

Terrified, Amrita pulled herself free and dashed through the open door of a dilapidated house. She pushed the ancient door shut and leaned dizzily against it. There was a nasty smell of rotting garbage and old wet rags. Her feet squelched in the muck making a sucking sound.

"I must get out." Amrita tried to open the door. It wouldn't budge. Amrita was locked in. She screamed and beat on the door but nobody could hear. Turning fearfully round she could hardly see in front of her. Once more she beat on the door, then sank to her knees sobbing with fright.

"Rupa," she screamed out, "Rupa!" Silence, then in the distance a faint bark. "Rupa! Rupa!"

Again an answering bark, louder this time. Then silence.

"Rupa," whispered Amrita, closing her eyes. A soft nose pushed at her arm. A hairy body pressed near to her. Amrita gave a shriek and almost fainted. The hairy thing gave another little bark. A dog! It was a dog. Slowly opening her eyes and lifting her head, Amrita looked fearfully at it.

Standing in front of her and quivering in delight at his unexpected find was a tough looking, medium sized dog, with short ginger fur. His bright amber eyes looked curiously at her. His pointy ears twitched as he gave several little woofs as if to say, I'm very pleased to meet you.

Amrita shrank back from it. Dogs bite. Rupa always told her to keep away from them. But this one looked friendly. What should she do? The samosa, Amrita remembered she had a samosa. Fumbling in her pocket, she took it out. The dog wagged his tail enthusiastically. Amrita threw the samosa on the ground. The dog sniffed delicately at it and gobbled it down. He then sat and looked at her, his tail gently thumping to and fro.

Amrita stared at it. She became more confident. Leaning over towards it, she whispered, "You've got to get me out of here. You found your way in, now can you take me out?" She nodded encouragingly at the dog. Staggering to her feet, she grabbed hold of the dog's fur.

The dog looked up at her and seeming to understand what she wanted, turned and picked his way through the garbage. Amrita clutched the dog tightly and stumbled with him.

The floor suddenly gave way to a gaping hole. Beams of wood had fallen haphazardly across it. Amrita could hardly see the other side. She let go of the dog and stood shaking by the hole. How could they cross?

The dog stepped onto one of the beams and trotted across. At the far side he yelped in encouragement to Amrita.

Seeing that she wasn't moving, he ran back across the beam and tugged at her skirt.

Amrita couldn't walk across. The beam was too narrow. She was scared. The dog pulled again at her skirt.

Amrita wanted to run back to the door, but then she had an idea. Feeling decidedly ill and dizzy, she sat down on the beam, gripped at it desperately and began to slowly lever herself along. The dog gave supportive whines as if to say keep going.

"Keep going! Keep going!" She said to herself as her hand slipped from the wet and filthy beam.

Slowly! Slowly! Amrita inched across, the dog waiting for her at the other side.

The other side! She'd reached the other side!

Amrita again grasped the dog and staggered along with him.

The wall had fallen down at the back of the building. Amrita and the dog clambered over the fallen bricks and down into a side alley. At the end was the noisy street. Amrita limped her way to it. One of her toes had caught on a sharp stone and was hurting. Where was she? She caught sight of an alleyway opposite and realised it was the one she'd walked down coming from the shack.

Without thinking she fled across the busy road missing cars, bikes, taxis lorry's and buses all by inches. She scarpered up the alleyway and back home.

Falling through the opening of the shack, she lay exhausted on the floor. Her eyes were screwed tightly shut.

A tentative bark made her open them. Two bright eyes,

two pointy ears and a black quivering nose poked through the flap.

"Go away!" yelled Amrita sitting upright. Rupa mustn't know what happened, she told herself. She'd be so cross and worried if she knew that Amrita had tried to follow her.

"Go away!" she said again. The dog looked at her and gave a short bark. The he retreated.

Amrita's lip trembled. How could she be so cruel? He'd been a very good and kind dog and now she had sent him away. Never mind, perhaps he would come back.

Rupa returned sometime later very pleased with herself. She'd found lots of old clothes stuffed into sacks. They had been dropped or dumped. Rupa hadn't wasted time finding out. She hauled the sacks round to the paymaster and he'd given her a good price for them. She lay down on a mattress and pushed some cartons of food to Amrita.

"Have you been alright?" she asked her

"Oh yes!" answered Amrita "I've been ok Rupa."

"You can come with me soon," continued Rupa.

"I'll be a good help."

"Yes, I know you will. You are a very good girl Amrita."

Amrita smiled, then she thought of the dog and gave a little frown.

Next day, after Rupa had set off on her rubbish search, the dog appeared again. This time Amrita was delighted to see him. At last she had a playmate.

THE SPIRIT OF GANESH

The dog seemed to know when Rupa had gone because every day he appeared just after she had turned down the alleyway.

First a black quivering nose would push through the plastic sheeting then the dog would bound into the shack. His body wriggled with delight as he saw Amrita waiting expectantly for him. He would bounce up to her licking her face and whining in excitement. Amrita would pretend to push him off.

"Go away!" she would say in a stern pretend voice. "Go away you bad dog."

Scrabbling under the mattress she would pull out some scraps of food she had hidden for him. He would gobble them down and then roll over onto his back and Amrita would tickle his tummy.

"What can I call you?" She asked him one day, stroking his fur whilst he looked adoringly at her. "You should have a name. I'll have to think of one."

One morning, Mrs. Dhaliwall peeped into the shack to check that Amrita was alright. She saw the dog.

"Get that dog out Amrita!" she shrieked. "It's got fleas and rabies." Amrita flung her arm round him protectively, "He's a nice, friendly dog Mrs. Dhaliwall."

"Rupa would be furious of she knew." Mrs. Dhaliwall gave a sudden moan of pain and clutched at her side.

"Dhanvantari" she exclaimed. "I've got to go to pray to Dhanvantari."

"Dhanvantari?"

"The God of healing Amrita. I've got this pain and I hope Dhanvantari will cure it. Now shoo that dog out Amrita. I'll be back soon."

She hobbled off, pulling her scarf over her head and grasping at her side.

"Dhanvantari," Amrita paused and wrinkled her brow. "Dhanvantari? That's a good name but a bit long, she said aloud to herself. "Dan, Dan, Danva" she repeated it slowly "Danva, Danva? I like that, would you like to be called Danva?" she murmured to the dog, pulling him close to her.

"The God of healing," she whispered. "Well you made me better Danva. I'm never sad or lonely now."

The dog's ears pricked forward. He nuzzled up close to Amrita and wagged his tail. Amrita jumped up and with eyes sparkling with fun, held a piece of chapatti up. Danva leapt for it, where upon Amrita dashed out of the shack and round in circles. Danva barked and frantic efforts to catch it. Amrita laughed and threw it high into the air. Danva jumped and caught it in his mouth and swallowed it.

"Greedy dog!" Shrieked Amrita pushing him.

"Greedy, greedy dog!"

At this moment Rupa arrived home. "Amrita!" yelled Rupa. "What are you doing with that mangy dog? I told you to stay inside till I got back."

Amrita thought quickly. She didn't want Rupa to send Danva away, he was a very special dog.

"He came to play Rupa. He's been looking after me."

She didn't go into detail about the derelict house.

"Please! Please Rupa can he be our dog dearest sister Rupa? I've got a name for him it's Danva." Danva looked enthusiastically towards Rupa.

"How can we feed it?" asked Rupa distractedly.

Amrita sensed she was giving in.

"He finds his own food Rupa. Look he's not skinny. Please Rupa! Please!" her voice rose to a wail.

"Oh alright! Alright Amrita!" but keep him outside whilst we eat"

Amrita smiled secretly to herself. She leaned down to whisper in Danva's ear. "You're my friend and I love you."

17

A New Family

Rupa was exhausted. The rubbish man had only given her a few rupees for her collection. She leaned against the wall of the railway station wondering how she'd find the energy to stagger back to Amrita.

The sudden sounds of shouts and yells woke her from her sleepiness. Three rough youths were attacking a crippled boy in a cart. They tipped the cart over and pulled at the boy's shirt.

"Pay up!" they were shouting. Without thinking Rupa ran at them and leapt on the back of one of the gang. He elbowed her off and as she lay gasping on the pavement, he ran off with his mates.

Through the pain and shock, Rupa saw a young boy sitting next to her holding his head.

When he saw her looking at him he pulled himself to his overturned cart and attempted to push it away.

"Stop where are you going you're hurt. Your head bleeding."

The young boy appeared to be in shock. He shook his head.

"Where do you live?" again the boy pulled himself away and muttered something about living in the railway station.

Rupa contemplated the little sad figure in front of her and impulsively she said,

"Come back to our place and I'll clean you up."

The boy stared at her.

"What's your name?"

"Shanti", he said reluctantly. "Well, mine's Rupa and I have a little sister called Amrita, a dog named Danva and a home by the big church.

Amrita was sitting outside the shack with Danva waiting for Rupa. She scrambled to her feet when she saw Rupa pushing a truck with someone in it. Danva gave a soft warning growl.

"Who's this Rupa?"

"This is Shanti Amrita."

Santi frowned at Amrita and looked down at his torn shirt.

"I'm going to clean him up Amrita. He's been attacked by some bad boys."

It was after they had bathed his head and found him a clean top, the only spare one Amrita had, that Shanti began to cry. Tears fell down his cheeks. Amrita and Rupa stared at him.

"What is it Shanti?"

"What's the matter?"

"I've forgotten about Hamid. Oh, how could I forget him?" Shanti wailed, "I look after him. Just me! He's blind and he plays his flute by the entrance to the railway station. He won't move away until I get there." Amrita frowned and pulled at Rupa's sleeve. "We'll have to fetch him Rupa. We can't leave a blind boy all alone."

Rupa, exhausted, gazed at Shanti and Amrita who were both looking expectantly at her. Did she have any choice? She hesitated, then said in a sudden rush, "Well I'd better go and get him. You two stay here and wait."

With that she dragged herself back down to the station again.

In the shack Shanti was entertaining Amrita. He had pulled out a small wooden xylophone from his truck and, using two sticks, was making the most amazing music. He drew the sticks along the xylophone slats and ripples of water, raindrops and gentle winds wafted and swirled round the shabby room.

Amrita listened for a while completely entranced. Then leaping to her feet she whirled round in time to the bubbling and trilling sounds of the little wooden instrument.

Danva crept silently in and he too, unable to resist the music, threw back his head and howled.

At this moment, Rupa returned, holding the hand of a shy, handsome looking boy. His other hand clutched a flute. "Hamid!" shouted Shanti with delight. Hamid grinned down towards him. "Come in Hamid," continued Shanti "This is our home now with Rupa and Amrita," "and Danva," Amrita nudged Shanti, "And Danva the dog!" Shanti was overcome with happiness.

Hamid obediently sat down, still holding his flute tightly.

Rupa looked at the three of them. How was she going to feed them all? "I'll just go out and get some rice and dhall," she said tiredly, thinking of the few rupees she'd got from the rubbish man.

"We've got some rupees Rupa, you can have these as well."

Hamid fumbled about inside his shirt and handed the coins to Rupa.

"Ten! How did you get so much?"

We play our instruments and people like our music. They throw us money." Shanti grinned at Amrita. She nodded, smiling back at him.

Rupa contemplated the happy faces of the children. She and Amrita were not alone now. They were part of a family and she, Rupa, had to be Mother to all three of them. Shanti and Hamid could earn good money. Perhaps Amrita would be able to go to school.

There was a small bark from outside the shack. And they had a guard dog called Danva. Rupa stroked the small statuette of Ganesh in her pocket. Things were getting better.

There was a lightness in Rupa's step as she skipped down the alleyway to get the food for supper.

It was some days later that Mrs. Dhaliwal gave Rupa a crumpled envelope with a letter inside.

"A boy brought this Rupa," she told Rupa. "He said an old lady called Mrs. Choudery had given it him to give to you."

"Mrs. Choudery?" Rupa pulled a face trying to remember the name. "But I can't read Mrs. Dhaliwall. Can you read it for me?"

Mrs. Dhaliwall pulled out a creased sheet of paper from the envelope.

"It looks old Rupa. She attempted to smooth the paper and hesitantly began to read.

Dear Rupa

I trust this letter will reach you because I have no idea where you are.

We are still in Saudi Arabia and I continue my studies. Soon I will attend university to become a children's doctor.

I hope that you have Amrita safe. She is my inspiration. I pray every morning that I will some day find you.

I love you both

From Aisha

"Aisha!"

"Yes. I do have Amrita safe, Aisha. One day with Ganesh's help we will find each other again.

We love you too." from Rupa,